"Cache McKendrick, Lone Tree Ranch."

"Cash? Is that how you pay for everything?" Holly reached out a hand to shake his formally.

"No, darlin', Cache is short for Cachon, an old family name."

"I see." She swallowed. "Cache, then. I am not your darling, nor do I plan to be, so I think you should refrain from using that endearment."

That settled, she marched by him and headed for her Jeep.

Barbara McMahon was born and raised in the South, but settled in California after spending a year flying around the world for an international airline. Settling down to raise a family and work for a computer firm, she began writing when her children started school. Now, feeling fortunate in being able to realize a long-held dream of quitting her "day job" and writing full-time, she and her husband recently moved to the Sierra Nevada area of California, where she finds her desire to write is stronger than ever. With the beauty of the mountains visible from her windows, and the pace of life slower than the hectic San Francisco Bay Area where they previously resided, she finds more time than ever to think up stories and characters and share them with others through writing.

Books by Barbara McMahon

HARLEQUIN ROMANCE
2777—BLUEBELLS ON THE HILL
2895—WINTER STRANGER, SUMMER LOVER
3221—ISLAND PARADISE
3369—WANTED: WIFE AND MOTHER

Living For Love
Barbara McMahon

Harlequin Books

TORONTO • NEW YORK • LONDON
AMSTERDAM • PARIS • SYDNEY • HAMBURG
STOCKHOLM • ATHENS • TOKYO • MILAN
MADRID • WARSAW • BUDAPEST • AUCKLAND

ISBN 0-373-17263-X

LIVING FOR LOVE

First North American Publication 1996.

Copyright © 1994 by Barbara McMahon.

CHAPTER ONE

HOLLY reached into the back of the shiny new eggshell-blue jeep Renegade and drew out the last box. This one was the heaviest; it contained all the books she'd brought. She paused before lifting it, to gather her strength; she was tired.

The drive had been long and hot up California's central valley, across the mountains and into the Sierra Valley. She'd been on the road in the heat all day. Arriving only an hour ago in Waxco, she'd unloaded everything, stacking the boxes in the front room; this one was the last. But she still had to unpack and put things away. And fix something for dinner.

She rubbed her hands on her faded denim shorts, blew an errant strand of brown hair from her eyes and prepared to lift the carton when she heard another vehicle turn off the main road and into her short driveway.

Glad to put off moving the last box, she turned to watch as a beat-up old pick-up truck pulled in near her jeep, the engine died and the driver's door was thrust open. Holly watched curiously as a tall cowboy unwound from the truck and slammed the door, crossing the short distance between them smoothly, his eyes running a bold appraisal down her figure.

Warmth exploded through her, and then a strange excitement. Holly frowned, angry at herself for reacting to the stranger's look. Other men had given her that blatant provocative look before. She'd always ignored

5

them, as she should ignore him. Why did his look cause
her to feel as if she was the most attractive woman in
the world? Especially looking as she did—hot, tired and
dusty. She drew herself up to her full five-foot-two-inch
height and, acting as if she were ignoring the stranger,
turned back to the jeep, reaching for the box. If she was
to have company, she wanted to go inside, and didn't
want to waste the trip.

'Here, darlin', let me take that; it's too heavy for you.'

The voice drawled. There was no other way to describe it. Holly turned around as fast as the heavy load
would allow and stared up at him. Was he putting it on?

He was rugged, muscular and lean, no fat on this man.
His shirt displayed his broad shoulders, the sleeves rolled
back to reveal deeply tanned arms. A quick glance
showed that his jeans moulded his legs, worn on the insides as if from long hours in the saddle. His scruffy
cowboy boots were dusty and worn. Dragging her gaze
upwards, she met his look, finding his eyes laughing
down at her while the creases near his mouth proved he
smiled a lot. She couldn't see his hair, it was hidden by
the cowboy hat, nor could she tell the colour of his eyes
in the shadows beneath the rim of his hat. But she bristled
at his laughter.

'I can manage,' she said, taking a step towards the
porch.

'No, I'll carry it.' With no more said, he effortlessly
lifted the heavy box from her hands and tucked it beneath one arm as if it weighed nothing. Holly lifted her
eyebrows in surprise, thought better of arguing, and
turned to lead the way into the house, her visitor right
behind her. The box was no lightweight, yet he handled

it as if it were full of tissue paper. She was impressed in spite of herself.

Holding the screen door, she motioned to the stack of boxes near by and nodded. 'Thank you, you can put it there.'

He complied, and swept the hat from his head. Running his fingers through the dark blond hair revealed, he turned to assess her. His eyes were a dark blue, almost navy, slightly insolent in their regard from his lofty height. His skin was tanned a dark mahogany, his blond hair streaked with white. He smiled as his eyes travelled down her, and his teeth were startling white against his dark tan.

'Looking for the doc,' he said, glancing around. His voice fascinated Holly; it was deep, rich and lazy. It reflected the way he moved. Yet she detected a certain leashed energy, one that was harnessed, but could be let loose if needed. She stared a moment listening to the echo of his voice in her mind.

'Doc Watson's replacement,' he said again, his eyes roaming over her face, again down her body. Just so he'd be able to describe her if anyone asked about her, he told himself, liking what his eyes saw. The trim body, the long, tanned legs showing beneath the short, snug denim shorts, the pretty brown hair.

Cache McKendrick wondered who she was. A quick glance to her left hand reassured him. She wore no rings. There was an unfamiliar tightening in his gut, but he ignored it. Later he'd take the time to learn who she was, why she was in Waxco. He hoped she was the doctor's sister, and not his wife. But for now he needed the doctor, not some beautiful woman no taller than his shoulder with rich, wavy brown hair, eyes the colour of fine brandy, and a trim figure that cried out for a man's touch.

'You've found me,' Holly said, disturbed by his survey. Her nerve-endings were tingling, she felt as if he had reached out and touched her. His eyes were intense, his scrutiny thorough. She willed herself to remain calm and to ignore the feelings he caused, but her heart pounded faster than normal and she felt warmer than she had on the long car drive up. She longed to put some distance between them, but held her ground. She would not be intimidated by some brash cowboy. She was the new vet, and it sounded as if he needed a vet.

There was something blatantly sexual about the man, from his arrogant stance to the snug fit of his jeans, to the way his eyes boldly travelled over her body. He was the most compelling, *masculine* male she'd ever seen. And she was used to being around men, from her uncle and cousins through to colleagues of her profession. But never had she been so physically aware of a man before. She was fascinated by him and her reaction.

She felt feminine, desirable, and suddenly very interested in learning more about the man before her.

He frowned, his eyes narrowed and he glanced quickly around as if looking for someone else. Anyone else. He looked at her again, the laughter gone from his eyes, his face serious and determined.

'You can't be. Doc Watson said he'd gotten a locum in for the time he's gone, a Doc Murphy—H. Murphy.'

Holly stood tall, tilting her chin slightly, and nodded crisply. 'That's right, I'm Dr Holly Murphy, standing in for Dr Watson. What can I do for you?'

'Damnation.' He said the word softly, almost as a sigh, but Holly stepped back, not liking the way he looked at her. He shook his head, frustration showing for the first time.

'There's been a mistake, darlin'. You go on back to the city and watch out for the cats and dogs you're used to. We need a large animal vet up here. Not some pretty little thing used to Pekinese pups.' His eyes were hard, his tone disgusted.

Holly bristled instantly. 'Now just a minute, cowboy. Before you jump to any conclusions, you need to get your facts straight. I am a large animal vet. I specialise in cattle and equines. I'm just as good a vet as your Doc Watson.' She tilted her chin up at him, her eyes snapping at the implied judgement that she couldn't do the job just because she was a woman. She'd been proving herself for years now, and this opinionated, *masculine* cowboy wouldn't be the one to find her lacking. Maybe she exaggerated just a little when saying she was as good as Dr Watson—she didn't have the years of experience that doctor had. But she knew what she was doing. She had done well in school, was fully qualified, had been in practice for several years.

'You're not big enough,' he countered, his eyes drifting over her again, lingering on the shapely curves the shorts displayed, lingering on the honey-gold of her skin, the trim ankles, muscular calves. His eyes met hers again and he shook his head.

'I'll get Stan over from Overilla.'

'Who's Stan?' she asked, wondering just who this cowboy thought he was to pass judgement on her abilities sight unseen. Would she find this kind of blatant distrust throughout the area just because she was a woman?

'Stan Connors is the vet over in the next county. He can help me out.' He turned to go.

Holly reached out her hand impulsively and stopped him as he was turning. His skin was warm, the muscles on his forearm tight and firm. Holly was surprised at the tingling that flooded through her when she touched him, but refused to let that slow her down. She took a sharp breath and held on to her determination; he wanted a vet, he had one. Her.

'Just a minute, cowboy. I'm a fully qualified vet. What do you need, Mr...?' She trailed off; she didn't even know who he was.

Cache felt her touch like a feather, like the lightest breeze across the land, yet he also felt the shock of her skin against his. His eyes narrowed as he watched her. He could feel her determination, her tenacity, the sheer strength of her resolve as she stared up at him. For a moment he wavered.

Hell, he could always have her out to see the damn horse. Once she'd seen what she would be facing, she'd back off and he'd call Stan; there was time. The situation was serious enough to warrant a vet, but not yet a crisis.

'I have a mare ready to foal soon. She's old and not due yet. Today she injured her leg. I need a vet to check her out.' He couldn't explain his capitulation, and frowned down at her, not wanting to question it even to himself.

'I'll be ready in two seconds.'

Holly turned and hurried to her bedroom. Flinging her heavy suitcase on the bed, she threw it open and rummaged around for a pair of jeans. Donning an old but serviceable pair, she scrambled into her hiking boots and grabbed a long-sleeved jacket. All the normal attire for working around barns, and large animals. It got cool in the evenings, thus the jacket. She glanced around at the suitcases in the room, and thought of the boxes in the next room. She'd have to unpack tomorrow; no telling how long she'd be tonight. And no dinner either.

Impatiently, she checked her watch. She'd only been gone five minutes. Was the cowboy still there? Or had he taken that time to disappear? She almost held her breath as she threw open the bedroom door.

He was standing near the door, looking around the room, examining her boxes as if wondering what each contained. She paused a moment, taking the time to study him a little more. He looked out of place in the living-room, more like he belonged to the great out-doors. He was absently turning his hat in his hands, trying to read the labels on her boxes. Her heart lightened; she was suddenly glad he'd waited.

'Ready,' she said crisply, businesslike. She knew her looks often went against her. The long hair that waved around her face was easily tied back when she was working, she wore very little make-up, but with her dark eyebrows and lashes, and the smoothness and colour of her complexion, she needed very little. She didn't pay much attention to her looks. She was more interested in becoming a good vet. But she knew her looks and diminutive stature sometimes fooled others into thinking she wasn't up to her profession.

'That was fast.' He checked out her attire as she grabbed her bag. His feelings were mixed. The jeep and the black satchel she carried were brand-new. He felt somewhat mollified by the obvious use the hiking boots and jeans had seen. Maybe she did know what she was doing. But she was still too small. And too damned pretty.

In fact, she looked too small even to carry that heavy head of hair. Though he wished he could lift a strand or two of the warm brown tresses to see if it felt as silky to the touch as it looked.

He stepped back abruptly. 'Never did introduce myself. Cache McKendrick, Lone Tree Ranch. East of town.'

'Cash? Is that how you pay for everything?' She reached out a hand to shake his formally. His fingers tightened over hers; she could feel the calluses in his palms. She hadn't expected the small shock when their hands clasped. As quickly as she could, she withdrew hers.

His smile was lop-sided, and arrogant, but the creases in his cheeks deepened and his eyes danced in amusement at her guess. Had he noticed the reaction she'd felt? He nodded for her to precede him from the house and pulled the door shut behind him, giving nothing away.

'No, darlin', Cache is short for Cachon, an old family name. John Cachon McKendrick's the full name. Most folks call me Cache. My dad's called John.'

'I see.' She swallowed. Was she to call him Cache? Would he call her Holly?

'I can follow you out, save you bringing me back,' she said as she led the way to the vehicles.

'Wouldn't be a bit of trouble, darlin',' he said, giving her another grin.

'Mr McKendrick . . '

'Cache.'

'Cache, then. I am not your darling nor do I plan to be, so I think you should refrain from using that endearment.' That settled, she marched by him and headed for her jeep. It would never do to have him find out the curious tingle she experienced deep within her heart when he called her that. She'd never in her life had anyone call her darling and for a moment she wistfully wished she were someone's darling.

Straightening her shoulders, she put that thought behind her. She was doing what she wanted and at the end of this assignment she would be returning home at last—finally proving to her family that she could make it on her own and then being accepted by them as a competent professional. Time enough for relationships after that hurdle was overcome.

'Whatever you say, darlin',' McKendrick said softly just as she reached the car. When she glared over at him she met his laughing eyes. Lips tight with displeasure, Holly got into the jeep and slammed the door, wondering if anyone ever got the last word with him.

Cache backed his truck out on to the road and roared away. Holly hurried after him, determined he wouldn't lose her on the way to the Lone Tree ranch.

She needed to get a map of the area and start learning her way around, but for now she was dependent on following him. She concentrated on keeping his tail-lights in sight. Not for anything would she give him reason to think she couldn't do the job, especially something as simple as following him to his ranch.

He drove just as he appeared, she thought as they sped down the highway, reckless, arrogant and dangerous. His truck looked old, battered and most disreputable, but it obviously had a good engine because she was hard pressed to keep up with him. He held himself with a certain arrogance that showed everyone he was sure of himself, knew just who he was and liked it. She smiled for a second; she liked it, too. Frowning suddenly, she shook her head. There was no use getting interested in some cowboy. She was only in Waxco for six months. Then she would be going home.

It was over seven years since she'd last been home. Her lips tightened. Time enough to worry about changes later—worry about how her uncle Tyson would greet her when she was ready to return. She'd set out to prove herself and she had succeeded. At least to herself. Now she had to prove herself to her uncle. Then she'd know she had made it.

The truck ahead slowed and turned on to a long, narrow dirt road, fenced on both sides. Cache picked up speed again and Holly matched him mile for mile. When the buildings came into view, she spared them only a glance, following right behind the dirty truck as it drew to a sudden halt before a huge barn, dust settling softly as she drew up beside him.

To the right, several long yards away, a long, low ranch house faded into the twilight. It was set in a hollow, its sandy stucco and tile roof blended in with the land, as if it had belonged from the beginning. She spared it one more glance before looking back to the barn, and the corrals that flanked it. Horses were standing in both corrals, their heads raised to watch them. She smiled involuntarily; she loved horses. The barn was a big structure, built solid, with wide double doors left open.

Cache was at her door before she stopped fully, opening it for her, his face a bit uncertain. 'You sure you know what you're doing?' he asked as Holly drew her case from the seat beside her.

'Yes. Where's the mare?' She stood beside him, having to tilt her head back to see him. The brim of his cowboy hat still shaded his face, yet she could see his narrowed gaze as he stared down at her.

Shaking his head, he murmured, 'I'm a fool for a pretty face.' Slamming the jeep door, he turned and entered the barn. 'This way.'

She watched him as he walked away. Walked was the wrong word—his movement was a smooth as a wolf's when he was hunting prey, as arrogant as a stallion's when strutting before brood mares, as unconcerned about others as she'd ever seen. Sashaying after him, she tried to emulate his rolling gait, but knew after only a few steps that she didn't have it. Couldn't do it. Shaking her head at her fanciful nonsense, she entered the dimmer light of the big barn.

Cache was already halfway down the aisle. Box stalls ranged on both sides, the loft opened in the middle, sweet-smelling hay stacked up several bales high. Easy to feed the horses in the stalls below. Holly noticed that only a few stalls had occupants; most of the horses were out in the corrals Holly had seen when they first drove up.

Cache was not alone when Holly finally reached him. Two other cowboys were standing by the stall, leaning on the door, watching an older man in the stall with the mare.

Holly paused a moment, then unlatched the half-door and slipped inside. She was the vet, and had better take charge before Cache changed his mind and called the one from Overilla.

The mare was lying on her side, obviously swollen with pregnancy. The old man was stroking her neck and crooning to her when Holly squatted beside him.

'How is she?' she asked softly, her eyes taking in the situation. She could see the swelling in her foreleg, but that wasn't causing the mare's problems. She was in labour. Early labour, if Cache's earlier pronouncement was correct.

'Who are you?' the old man asked in surprise of the young girl who stepped in with him.

'She's the new doc.' Cache joined them in the stall. 'Doc Watson's replacement. Is she in labour?'

Holly knew he wasn't referring to her, and she ran experienced hands over the mare.

'Yes.'

'I'll call Stan.' Cache turned, only to be caught up again by Holly's hand firm on his arm.

'You go call whomever you want, Mr McKendrick. But I'm going to help this horse. And once another vet finds out a qualified vet is on-site, he won't rush over to butt in.' She hoped that was true. What was she going to have to do to prove to this arrogant man that she could do the job? She couldn't let her first assignment be passed over to someone else—she'd never be able to gain the trust of the town.

'You two going to jaw all day, or help this pore horse?' The old man stood up and looked over to them. Holly turned and saw that he was tall, taller than Cache, and thin as a rail. A good wind would likely blow him away.

'I'm here to help the mare. When did this start?' Holly was all business. She couldn't help what McKendrick might do. All her energy now had to be focused on helping this horse. Holly remembered Cache had told her the mare was old, and this labour came just after she'd been injured. Her strength would be down. She needed to deliver and be tended to before it became too much for her.

'You're not strong enough if any heavy work needs to be done,' McKendrick said to her back.

She threw him a look, running her gaze down the length of him, and knew it had been a mistake. No one could possibly wear jeans that tight and not have them painted on. They were worn and faded and soft and moulded his long legs like a second skin. They fitted him like a glove, revealing the strong muscles of his thighs, and all his masculine splendour. She dragged her gaze back to his face, only to meet his knowing, amused eyes.

'You've got the brawn, and in this case I've the brains to know what needs to be done. You can help if I can't do it alone.'

Cache nodded. He was amused by her obvious interest in him, and yet relieved to find she wasn't so hard-headed that she'd insist she could do everything herself. He didn't mind being the brawn, especially if it gave her second thoughts about him. Though he knew she would never admit such a thing right now. Maybe, given time. In the meantime, he knew a thing or two about animals, too. Maybe between them they could save Sunlight. If not, it would not be because he didn't give the new doctor every chance.

But, he sighed as he went to stand beside her, he hoped he wasn't sacrificing one of his favourite mares just to have the doctor prove a point. He wished Doc Watson were still in town.

Hours later Holly smiled tiredly at the spindly-legged foal that tottered near his mother. She leaned against the stall wall and watched, almost too hungry and tired to move. She wondered if she could even stay awake long enough to drive home. In only a moment she would leave; she wasn't needed here any longer. But for now she would just watch the new baby and his mother; she was too tired to do anything else.

It had been a long session. First she'd fixed up the leg, then worked with Cache to monitor the mare's progress. When the foal needed help, it was Holly who directed Cache just where to place his hands beside hers, she who had given him the directions as they worked together as a team to assist in the birth.

During the long hours, Cache had joked with his fellow cowboys, told stories, swapping yarns between them, designed, Holly suspected, to keep her mind off the difficulty of the birth and focused on the amazing exploits of these men. Most of them tall tales, she was sure, but they did make her feel more at ease. It had been a thoughtful thing to do, and she glanced at Cache, wondering if her assessment of him was entirely correct. Was there more to him than brash, cocky cowboy?

She smiled again and looked at the men. They didn't look as tired as she felt, thought it would soon be dawn and Cache had worked alongside her the entire time. They were pounding each other on the back, congratulating themselves on the new birth as if it had been their idea.

She smiled at the mare; where was the credit for Mama? The horse was now standing, favouring her injured leg, nuzzling her new offspring. Some of Holly's tiredness faded watching them. This was the happy part of her work.

Cache caught her look and hunkered down beside her. 'Should give the mare credit for a little of it, eh?' His hat was shoved back on his head, his face near hers. She could see the lines that fanned out by his eyes, evidence of the long hours he spent in the hot California sun. The deep dark blue of his irises, the clear white...

She nodded and looked away, disconcerted that he seemed to read her mind.

'She did do most of the work,' she murmured, wondering how she would find the strength to stand, much less get home. She was even too tired to look at her watch. How late was it?

'Darlin', I take back every suspicious thought I had about you. You did real good.' His breath ruffled across her cheek, his eyes smiled down at hers. For a second Holly wondered what would happen if she leaned forward just a little bit and let her lips brush across his.

Her eyes widened at the thought, heat washed through her. Where were her wits? Was she so tired she'd fallen asleep and was dreaming?

Cache's smile faded as he stared into her brandy-coloured eyes. She had been here for hours, yet appeared as cool and serene and as scrubbed as if she'd just left her place. Her skin was creamy, smooth like honey, her hair dark and soft, highlights glinting in the artificial light, pulled back with a string they'd found for her. He longed to release the tie and let her hair swirl about her face the way it had when he'd first seen her that afternoon. He still wondered if it felt as soft as it looked.

Abruptly he frowned and stood up. Offering his hand, he reached down to pull Holly to her feet, his hand impersonal around hers.

'Thanks, Doc, how much do I owe you?' His voice was cool, abrupt.

She blinked, so sudden was the change. She glanced around the barn; no one else had seen anything amiss; had she imagined his sudden change? One moment friendly, the next withdrawn and remote.

'I'll send a bill. I guess I'll head for home now. I can come tomorrow and check on them both, but I think they'll do fine.' She wouldn't leave if she thought either was in danger. But she wanted something to eat and her bed.

Slowly Holly packed up the equipment she'd used and snapped her case closed. She still had to walk to her car and drive home. She couldn't wait to get some sleep. Taking a deep breath, she turned and smiled coolly.

'If you can just tell me how to get home, that is. I turn left on the main road, don't I?'

'I can take you home, Doc,' the old man said. His name was Sam. Holly had had the chance during the night to learn all their names, and a bit of what each did. She didn't know much about Cache, though. Except that he could tell a tall tale with the best of them.

'I'll see her home.' Cache's voice was low and firm.

'Sure, whatever. Thanks, Doc.' Sam grinned at her and at Cache, but looked away when the younger man glared at him.

'Bye for now,' Holly said to the others, Tim and Larry. They had been at Lone Tree Ranch for several years, though Sam had been there the longest. How long Cache had been there she still didn't know. Was he deliberately being vague about himself?

And why did she care? She had done her job and was now ready to head for home. If they needed a vet, she'd be back. Otherwise, she wouldn't likely see them again any time soon.

She walked to her still shiny new jeep, conscious of how conspicuous it was in the yard with dirty, dusty trucks, of the hay clinging to her jeans, the weariness that went straight through to every bone in her body. She was hot, sticky and tired, so tired. It had been such a long day. Packing last night, getting up early to drive to Waxco. Then the delivery. She raised her hand to pull off the string she'd used to tie back her hair. The ranch had installed lights in the barnyard, and it was as light out as it had been in the barn.

The tie knotted. She tugged, but nothing happened. With a sigh, she gave up. She was too tired to fight it. She'd wait until she got home and cut it off.

'Here, I'll get it loose.' Cache's voice sounded just over her left ear. She felt his fingers working the errant string, then felt the release as he worked the knot loose and let her hair spill down. She stiffened as his fingers lingered for a moment, trailing the strands of her hair through them, and then releasing her.

Only then did Holly realise she had been holding her breath.

'Thank you.' Her voice was soft, faint. She turned and leaned against the jeep, her legs not as strong as she would wish.

'I think I can get home fine. You don't need to show me the way; I think I remember from yesterday afternoon.'

He grinned down at her. 'No problem. I'll lead the way.'

Her eyes narrowed in suspicion. 'If I were Doc Watson, would you show him the way home?' She didn't want any special treatment just because she was a woman. If the local ranchers thought she couldn't do the job without special treatment, they'd never call her for assistance. She needed to succeed in this job before she could go home; it was important to her.

Cache rested a forearm on the jeep-top, his body very near Holly's. Her throat tightened. He was so close. She could smell the masculine scent of him, the hay they'd been sitting on, the slightly musky smell of dried perspiration and sunshine. And the tangy scent of horse. It was not unpleasant and she drew in a deep breath, her senses aware of him as she'd never been aware of anyone before. He was too close.

'Now, darlin', I didn't have to show Doc Watson the way home 'cause he was in this part of the country before I was. But you're new, and I sure don't want you getting lost leaving the Lone Tree. We have a reputation for hospitality to uphold.'

'But I do remember the way.' Was he doing it deliberately, getting so close she could scarcely think? His shoulders were broad, muscular, straining the cotton shirt he wore. His arm was so brown, as was his face and neck. Was he that rich mahogany tan all over? She bit her lip. She was acting like a giddy schoolgirl with her first crush.

Cache stared down at her for a long moment, then nodded abruptly and stood back. 'OK. Thanks for coming.'

That's it? she thought as she climbed into the jeep and quickly started the engine. She'd expected more of an argument, more of his sweet-talking to try to convince her that he should see her home. And to what purpose? She could remember the way. It was almost a straight shot from this ranch to the edge of town where she was staying in Dr Watson's house.

As she backed around in the yard and headed out the way she'd come in, she wondered if perhaps he'd wanted to take her home and stay a while. She shook her head. Foolish thoughts. Men like him probably had women lined up. He wouldn't waste his time with someone like her. And especially not as she was tonight. She wanted only to get home and take a shower and go to bed.

But another night she might like to have him come in.

CHAPTER TWO

WHEN Holly let herself into the house, she noticed that the answering machine was blinking. She hurried over and rewound the tape and sank beside the phone to listen, propping her head up on her hand, elbow on the desk. She hoped it was not an emergency, that she didn't have to go out again tonight. She was exhausted.

A soft-spoken voice let her know that Emmie Haslet had tried to reach her. She was Doc Watson's nurse and would be coming by the office first thing in the morning. She hoped Doc Murphy was settling in OK.

There were no other messages, so Holly gratefully reset the machine and went to get ready for bed. As she ran the water for her shower, she took in a deep breath. She was lucky to get this job, for six months.

Dr Watson had explained his practice to Holly when she'd first applied for the position as locum in his absence. He and his wife were taking a long-awaited vacation. Their first one in years. For six months. They planned to visit all their children, who lived in various places in the US. Then they were going on a cruise.

While Holly had never spoken directly to Dr Watson, his letters had been very explicit and informative. She had kept them all and planned to use them for reference if she found the need.

His practice was located in the town of Waxco, but he was on call to the various ranches in the area. There was an occasional family in town that had a dog or cat,

24

but most of his practice centred on the cattle ranches surrounding Waxco.

Emmie was his nurse, assistant, office manager and general factotum, as far as Holly could tell from his background correspondence. According to one of Dr Watson's letters, Holly could rely entirely upon Emmie to give her all the information she needed concerning the patients in the practice.

As the hot water beat down on her tired back, Holly smiled a little in anticipation of meeting Emmie. As far as she knew, before Cache McKendrick met her this afternoon, no one knew the replacement doctor would be female. Would Emmie be as sceptical about her as Cache had been? And if so, what would Holly have to do to prove herself to Emmie?

Drying off, she carefully reviewed everything she'd written. In no correspondence had she made mention of the fact that she was a woman, but she also had never actually lied about it, or claimed that she was a male. She knew, however, the general consensus would be that veterinarians were men.

That was what her uncle had told her. All her life she'd wanted to work on Windmere Farms as a vet. To work with the horses her uncle raised and raced. Her cousins worked there. And since Holly's uncle raised her when her parents died, she'd assumed she would have the chance to work at Windmere. But each time Holly had suggested it, she'd been told firmly that it wasn't a woman's place to do that; her job was to have a good time, and let the men take care of her.

She turned off the light and slid beneath the covers in the guest-room bed. It felt heavenly to lie down, stretch out and relax her muscles. She set her alarm for seven-thirty, wanting to get up early and get dressed at least before Emmie arrived at eight. It had been a long first day.

As Holly negotiated the turn on to the long drive leading to Lone Tree Ranch the next afternoon, she reviewed her morning. From the first when she'd tried to decide how to dress to meet Emmie, standing before the mirror, trying to judge whether her blue checked cotton shirt and clean jeans were appropriate. Or whether she should wear her white lab coat over the jeans. She'd tried it on. Throwing her stethoscope around her neck, she'd looked a physician. Yanking the stethoscope off, she had left on the coat; it did give some air of authority. But were they more casual in Waxco than elsewhere? What did Dr Watson wear?

The knock at the front door had interrupted her musings. She'd left on the coat, stuffed the stethoscope in her pocket and hurried to answer it.

Holly smiled when she thought of Emmie Haslet. What a character. Was everyone in town odd in one way or another? Emmie was even smaller than Holly herself. She must be seventy if she was a day, and hadn't blinked an eye when she'd seen Holly was a woman. Welcomed her, led her to the office and reviewed the set-up with Holly. Emmie had given Holly the pager that Doc Watson used and logged in the visit Holly had made to the Lone Tree ranch.

Emmie had strongly concurred when Holly suggested she might want to follow up and see how the mare and her foal were doing.

'I agree, Doc. This afternoon. Just to be neighbourly, you understand. Of course, I wouldn't suggest it normally, but since Sunlight was injured, and her being one of Cache's favourites and Cache being so influential and all.'

Just the mention of Cache McKendrick's name had Holly remembering his smile, the way his eyes crinkled, the deep tone of his voice. His calling her 'darlin''. Her heart had sped up and she'd turned away lest Emmie see something Holly didn't want anyone to suspect. But just who was Cache so influential with? All the women in town?

She drove along the same route he'd led her down yesterday. Ahead she could see the same pick-up truck, pulled off the drive at an odd angle. Had he run off the road?

She slowed, then pulled to a stop near the truck. Cache and another man were working on the fence lining the drive just a few yards ahead of the truck. Cache's hat was low on his face, but he had discarded his shirt. His shoulders and chest gleamed with a faint sheen of perspiration as he dropped a post-hole digger into the ground, worked the levers out and pulled up some of the hard clay.

Holly was glad she wore her dark glasses today; he would not be able to see where she was looking. And she was looking directly at him!

Her cousins both belonged to a health club and worked out several times a week just to get a physique like this one. They didn't even come close.

His jeans rode low on his hips, his stomach was flat and hard, his chest and shoulder muscles rippled as he worked. Only seconds after she stopped, he looked over to her. She could swear he looked directly into her eyes. With a quick word to the other man, Cache handed him the hole-digger and walked easily over to the jeep.

Holly watched him as he strode towards her, the same easy gait he'd used last night, smooth, controlled, almost fluid in its grace. She nodded through her rolled-down window as he approached and gave him a polite smile. It was all she could do to stop herself from grinning like a giddy teenager.

'Howdy.' Cache rested both forearms along the bottom of the window.

'Good afternoon. I—er—thought I'd come check on my first patients in Waxco. Both doing fine, I'm sure.'

'Sure thing. Both doing fine. 'Preciate your coming by, though. Might want to check on Sunlight's leg, too, see if it's mending all right.'

'Yes.' She should drive on, but was hesitant to leave. 'Aren't you hot out here?' she stalled.

The sun was past its zenith, but it was still extremely warm. Holly was used to the hot summers in California, but she tried not to work directly in the broiling sun. No wonder he was so tanned if he did this every day.

'Things are getting warmer. After you see to the mare and foal, care to stop over at the house for a lemonade or iced tea?' he asked, his eyes searching her face.

Her eyes drifted over Cache, drawn to his hard stomach, corded with muscles, down to the tight jeans he wore. She knew they couldn't fall off; they were too snug.

She felt warm, and it wasn't just the heat of the day. She swallowed hard.

'Maybe some other time. Emmie has me on a schedule to meet some of the people around, so they'll feel comfortable calling on me if they need a vet.'

He smiled, his teeth white and even and straight. Her eyes were drawn to his mouth and she couldn't look away. She licked her lips and with so doing drew his attention to them. When his smile faded Holly felt the very air charge with something she couldn't identify. His face was shaded by the hat, but she saw his eyes on her mouth, the amusement gone, and something else replacing it. Was it hunger?

'Well, I guess I'll go check on Mama.' She dragged her eyes away and moved to put the jeep in gear.

'I'll ride up with you. You can let me know if anything's wrong.' Cache had made the decision when she'd said she'd be going. For some reason, he didn't want her to go so soon. Calling over to the other man, he went around the car, opened the passenger door and slid in beside her.

Holly felt as if he filled her jeep. His presence seemed greater than the size of him warranted. She was aware of every inch of his body as she started off, could see him from the corner of her eye. His shoulders almost brushed against hers, his long legs looked cramped in the jeep.

'I could have given you a report on my way out,' she said nervously as she drove.

'Yep, but I wanted to see you in action again.'

'Still not convinced I'm qualified to provide medical services?' Her ire rose slightly.

He chuckled and turned halfway round in his seat, his left arm resting on the back of hers, the warmth from his skin crossing the space to Holly. She held herself still.

'You're sure a defensive little thing. Any remark that can be twisted around to imply you're not a good vet and off you go. Drop the chip off your shoulder, darlin', no one's challenging you here.'

'I told you yesterday not to call me that,' she snapped, annoyed that he'd criticised her attitude. She knew she was defensive, but she had to be; so few people took her seriously unless she pressed the issue. Her own family hadn't.

'Well, yes, ma'am, Dr Murphy, ma'am. I'll sure stop calling you that. What should I call you, ma'am?' He was mocking her, laughing at her and Holly's blood boiled.

'Just Dr Murphy will do,' she said frostily.

'Yes, ma'am, *Dr Murphy*.' He continued to watch her as she drove, that awful grin on his face, his eyes dancing with amusement.

Holly threw him a dirty look and wished she'd hurry up and reach the barn. He'd rubbed her up the wrong way, but when she'd reproached him for it she hadn't meant for him to laugh at her. She wished wistfully that she could capture some of the camaraderie from last night for herself. He spoke easily to the other cowboys, why not her?

Drawing up before the barn at last, Holly started to get out when Cache stopped her, his hand on her arm, moving to grasp her chin, tilt her face up to his.

'A word of advice, sugar. We're kindly folks hereabout. We help each other out, and rely on each other. Each person respects the other for what each one can do. If you're a good vet, we'll find out. You don't have to stand on airs and pretensions with us. Doc Watson gets on just fine with everyone and we all call him Doc. Or Harry, depending.'

Holly tried to listen to what he was saying, but it was hard. She could feel flames licking through her at the touch of his fingers along her jaw. Mesmerised by the serious look in his eyes, the deep tones of his voice, she was hard pressed to concentrate on what he was saying. And she didn't like it when she did.

Just who was he to preach to her? Some cowboy who tried flirting and didn't make it.

She jerked her head from his hand and nodded. 'Thanks for the lecture, cowboy. I'll keep it in mind.' She knew her tone was icy, but she was mad. And embarrassed that she'd needed to be told. She wanted to make this assignment work. She never wanted Dr Watson to regret giving her his practice while he was gone. And she wouldn't for anything alienate his patients. At least not the other ones. She feared that for this cowboy it was already too late.

Cache sat for another moment in the jeep, watching her walk into the barn, her back ramrod-straight, her head high. He could still feel the softness of her skin on his fingertips. He didn't remember ever touching someone so soft. Her hair last night had been like fine silk, her skin today as soft as a baby's. He growled deep in his throat and flung open the car door. He would not get caught up with *Dr Murphy*. She could do her work here and move on. He didn't care. She was nothing to him but the local vet. *Temporarily*.

Holly's eyes adjusted to the dimness of the barn as she walked along the centre aisle. It was quiet. The few horses that had been in last night were all out. As she approached Sunlight's stall, she could hear the soft shuffling of the horse in the hay. Reaching the door, she peered into the stall, her face lighting in happiness. The mare was on her feet, ears pricked forward as she watched Holly. Near her, quizzical eyes on her, the little chestnut foal balanced on his long, spindly legs.

'Saw you drive up, Doc. Came to check on our new babe, eh?' Sam came in from the other end of the barn. Holly smiled at him, feeling more as if she belonged, as if she already knew someone in Waxco.

'Yes.'

'Good on you. Shows you know what to do. Doc Watson always came by to check up, too.'

Holly nodded, looking guiltily back at the mare. If Emmie hadn't urged her to come, she wouldn't have thought it all that important. At her last practice, she had been on call for an English-riding academy and they were much more formal than Waxco. She was grateful for Emmie's advice, and would let her know it when she got returned.

'Dr Murphy plans to be the perfect vet, didn't you know?' Cache's voice reached every inch of the barn, dripping sarcasm, yet he hadn't raised his voice. Holly ignored him. She deserved it; she'd been rude to him and didn't know how to get on his better side, if he had one. Maybe she'd do best to ignore him from now on. If she didn't say anything, she would not give him food for more teasing.

'Now, boss, she is a right smart doc, for a woman.'

Holly let the slight pass by; she swung around and faced Cache. 'Boss? Are you the foreman of this place?' she asked in horror. There had been no mention of that last night. She didn't want to be in the position of ignoring the foreman of one of the biggest ranches around.

'Nope,' Cache said.

Sam chuckled. 'Nope is right. He owns the Lone Tree; didn't you know, Doc?'

Holly stared in disbelief at Cache. No wonder he was arrogant. He had reason to be. From what she'd seen, the Lone Tree was huge, and prosperous. He could strut around all over if he owned all this. And she'd thought him arrogant because of his good looks and physique. Emmie had been right, the owner of this ranch would be influential, and now Holly knew where—everywhere!

'Make a difference, Dr Murphy?' His voice was silky, his smile sardonic.

His tone fired her anger again. 'No, why should it? I'm still a vet, and you're still the most arrogant, brash, outrageous man I've ever met.'

Cache roared with laughter at her obvious frustration. Holly eyed him with hostility but prudently kept quiet. When he'd settled down to a chuckle, she gave him a dirty look and opened the stall door. Checking the mare and the foal quickly, she was satisfied that both were doing well. The leg was starting to heal, and the mare had come through the difficult delivery fine.

She was conscious that Sam and Cache stood by the door, watching her, yet neither spoke while she checked her patients. When she was finished, she looked at Sam, ignoring Cache.

'I'd say by tomorrow you can let them in the corral, as long as you keep them apart from the other horses.' She was only saying that to cover all bases; she knew these experienced ranchers wouldn't put the mare or foal in with the others just yet.

'Sure thing, Doc,' Sam said, looking from Holly to Cache. 'Be seeing ya, Doc.' He tipped his hat and walked out of the barn.

Holly let herself out of the stall, trying not to meet Cache's eye. She felt like a fool. How was she to know he was the boss of the whole operation? He could have mentioned it, and not laughed at her in front of Sam.

He was frustrating enough to drive a saint mad, and she was no saint.

'Thanks, Dr Murphy, for taking time to check on Sunlight.' His voice dripped sarcasm, as he turned to match her steps.

'Don't call me that!' she snapped, knowing he was deliberately goading her, yet unable to stop the flash of anger he evoked.

'Hell, don't call you this, don't call you that. Do you know what the hell you do want?' he asked as they headed towards the bright sunshine spilling into the barn from the large double doors, their steps muffled on the straw and packed earth.

She didn't answer.

'Well, I know what I want.' Before she could think of a reply, he pulled her to a halt and his head blocked the sunlight from her as he swept off his hat, leaned over and kissed her. His mouth was hot and firm against her lips, not dominating as she would have expected, but coaxing, tantalising, enticing. His lips moved against hers gently, yet exciting. Time stood still and bright sunlight danced against her lids as her pulse beat a rapid tattoo through her veins.

Holly tried to resist, but it was too much. She softened her lips, replied with pressure of her own. The sweet smell of the hay, the bright warmth of the sunshine spilling around them, the solid feel of the half-clad body beside her filled her senses. Her free hand came up and rested against his arm. She could feel the muscles tighten beneath her fingers, the hard strength of them, the warmth radiating from his skin.

When his lips drew back slowly, reluctantly, she wanted to stop him, keep him with her. But she stood still, silent.

Slowly opening her eyes, she saw his blazing down at her, all traces of amusement gone.

'Know what you want yet, Dr Murphy?' he asked, his voice soft and low.

Before she could reply, they heard the pick-up truck pull into the yard. Cache straightened and slammed his hat back on his head, moving purposely towards the sunlight.

Holly followed, watching him warily. What was his hurry? Didn't want to be caught compromising the vet by one of his employees? A kiss was fine, as long as no one knew? Well, she didn't want anyone knowing either!

When Holly emerged into the brightness of the yard, she saw Cache in deep conversation with the man she'd seen that morning working on the fence. Yet maybe the conversation wasn't so deep. Cache seemed to know when she came into the yard for he looked up, turning to lean insolently against the truck as he continued talking with the man, his eyes tracking her.

Feigning a disinterest she didn't feel, Holly tossed her head and marched purposefully to her jeep. Once safely inside, she donned her dark glasses. She felt protected, sheltered somewhat with them on. Glancing once at Cache, she could see he was still staring at her.

She started the car and gave a careless wave, proud of herself for the gesture. She watched him from her rear-view mirror as she slowly pulled away and headed back down the drive. He looked after her until the slight bend in the driveway hid him from view.

'Whew!' She let out a pent-up breath. She felt drained, exhausted, as if she'd run a mile or more. What was it about that arrogant, brash man that fascinated her so much? She'd met his kind before, usually all swagger and bull. But Cache seemed to back up the act with real accomplishments. The Lone Tree gave every evidence of being a prosperous ranch. Emmie had spoken highly of it and of Cache. Holly had suspected the older woman of trying a bit of matchmaking when suggesting that Holly visit this afternoon, but maybe she was genuine in her admiration of Cache and what he'd done.

When Holly reached her house, Emmie had gone. Finding a note tacked to the front door, she learned that Emmie would return before the end of the day. There had been only a few calls and Emmie had left a list of places Holly should visit that afternoon.

Letting herself into the cool house, Holly realised how hot it was outside. She was glad of a few moments' respite before heading out to meet her new neighbours. She got a large iced tea from the pitcher in the refrigerator and went to sit down.

The phone rang.

'Dr Murphy,' Holly answered crisply.

'Just wanted to make sure you got home OK,' a familiar voice drawled in her ear.

She swallowed, butterflies instantly churning in her stomach. Just the sound of his voice could make her forget everything. The memory of the kiss in the barn crashed around her.

'Thank you, I did.' Was that her voice, that soft, almost beguiling tone? She shook her head. Was she getting addled? She sat in the chair next to the desk, sipped her tea.

'There's a dance in town on Saturday. A bit fancy, and a lot of fun. Would you like to go with me?' Cache asked in that lazy don't-give-a-damn tone he had.

Holly froze. She had better put plenty of distance between herself and this man. She couldn't afford to get involved; she was the new vet and didn't want anyone thinking she was looking for favouritism from one of the leading ranchers. Besides, her goal was to return to Kentucky in a few months, not expand friendships in California.

'I don't think so,' she said slowly, curiously reluctant to refuse, knowing she should. He'd probably just take the time to poke fun at her at every turn, she tried to rationalise.

'Suit yourself. If you change your mind you know where I am, Dr Murphy.'

'Don't call me that,' she said sharply. He did it just to annoy her and he succeeded every time.

'You're sure a gal for saying don't. Bye, Doc.' With that he hung up the phone.

Holly held her end for a long moment, clutched against her breast. Wistfully she thought of a dance. It would be a nice way to meet people whom she wouldn't necessarily meet otherwise. Fit in a bit more. Slowly she replaced the receiver and finished her tea before starting her afternoon rounds.

For the next two days Holly was quite busy. She visited different ranches throughout the area, meeting the owners, meeting some of the cowboys and seeing sick animals, from horses and cattle to one little girl's sick pet rabbit.

She didn't see Cache McKendrick, nor any of his cowhands, but she thought of him a lot. At odd moments when she'd be driving, or when writing up her notes for the files, his tanned face would dance before her. She'd see his smile, the hat pulled low, or remember the strong shoulders and the way his muscles rippled as he worked on the fence.

On Thursday she had a light day. Returning home around three, she headed for the office and the files that awaited. Holly wanted everything to be up to date and in order for Dr Watson. She kept up with her paperwork on a daily basis, no matter how tired she was. Today she'd finish early and have a relaxing evening.

Emmie greeted her upon her return.

'You're back early. Get old Tom's sow fixed up?' Holly's last call had been to look after a sick sow for one of the furthest ranches in the area.

She smiled and nodded. 'For the time being. Mr Poplar sure is attached to that pig,' she murmured, drawing up the file and jotting down a couple of notes.

Emmie laughed softly. 'He is that. Ever since his wife died, that pig's become his family. He'll take it hard when she dies.'

'That won't be for a while yet,' Holly said. 'She's in good health, if he keeps her from the chocolate.'

'Wondered if that would be it. She's gotten into chocolate before.'

Holly scanned the file; there were two other notations similar to hers from Dr Watson.

'There's a dance in town on Saturday,' Emmie said, studying the young doctor, as she sat in a chair near the desk.

Holly kept her eyes firmly on the notes she was reading, the memory of Cache's invitation coming to mind. She had already regretted refusing a dozen or more times over the last couple of days.

'Be a shame to miss it,' Emmie added, fixing her pale blue eyes on Holly.

Holly looked up. 'Hmm?' she said, stalling.

'You should plan to go to the dance on Saturday. Meet some more people, some young people. Find a few friends so you feel more at home here,' Emmie said firmly. She might be tiny, but her personality was forceful and her energy level high. Holly gave up before she could be beaten.

'I might. Actually, I did get asked, but refused.' She toyed with the pen, refusing to meet Emmie's eyes.

Emmie's eyebrows raised and she stared at Holly, the question unspoken, yet loud between them. The silence stretched out, was too much; Holly grimaced slightly.

'It was Cache.'

'Cache McKendrick asked you to the dance, and you turned him down?' Emmie stared at her for a second, then smiled widely.

Holly nodded, not trusting that smile.

'Child, I can't remember the last time Cache asked anyone anywhere. He goes to everything, flirts up a storm, but has never brought anyone, never taken anyone home since Trish. And he asked you? He's one of the most prosperous ranchers in the area, big in the cattlemen's association, and you turned him down?'

'It doesn't mean anything. He was just trying to rile me,' Holly said defensively.

'Rile you? What for?'

'I don't know.' Holly looked away. She didn't want to go into everything with Emmie. It was bad enough that she had to remember what she'd said and Cache's reactions. She didn't need everyone else knowing about it.

Emmie sat for a moment, deep in thought. Finally she stood up and moved to get the phone and plop it before Holly.

'Call him now and say you'll go,' she ordered.

'I can't do that.' Holly was aghast. She'd had more and more moments of regret over the last few days that she'd turned him down, but she could never call him back and say she'd go with him. What if Emmie was wrong and he'd already asked someone else? She'd die of embarrassment.

'You can and will. It's a grand opportunity for you to meet everyone in town. And you'd have the stamp of approval of one of our leading ranchers. You're a fool if you don't make the most of this opportunity. Doc Watson would have.'

'Doc Watson would have gone with Cache?' Holly asked, with a shocked look on her face, knowing she was putting off the inevitable.

'None of your sass, girl, call him now. I'll leave, so you won't be self-conscious.' Emmie swept regally from the room. 'Mind you call right now,' closing the door with a finality that made Holly actually consider phoning him.

'Who's Trish?' Holly called after her. But there was only silence. Had Emmie heard her?

Holly stared at the phone. Dared she call Cache? She wondered what she could say, how he would react. Drawing the time out, she slowly looked up his number and stared back at the phone. Chances were that he'd be out somewhere, and not anywhere near his phone. Now would be the best time to call him. He would not be there and she could tell Emmie she'd tried. She could always go to the dance alone. Meet people by herself.

She froze at the thought. She wouldn't. She was too shy, too unsure of herself to walk into a hall full of people who'd known each other all their lives and try to introduce herself. Maybe she could go with Emmie. That woman wasn't afraid of anything. She could introduce Holly to everyone. See she met the young people. Emmie knew everyone in town; she'd know who Holly should meet.

That settled in her mind, she dialled the number wondering if she could hang up after only a few rings, or if she should at least let it ring a long time for show.

CHAPTER THREE

CACHE answered the phone on the second ring. Holly was stunned. She hadn't expected him to be there at all! For a moment her mind went blank, panic swept through her. She wiped one hand along her jeans, wishing she dared hang up.

'Hello?' His deep voice hadn't changed. She closed her eyes, immediately transported back to that morning in the barn; she could feel his lips on hers, the smell of hay and sunshine and male scent flooding her senses. She opened her eyes, blinked and took a deep breath.

'Hello, Cache? This is Holly Murphy,' she began. If he said anything to set her off, she would hang up on him!

'Hello.' His tone was soft, non-threatening.

'How are you?' she asked, stalling again. She just didn't know if she could go through with this. What if he laughed at her indecision? He'd already laughed at other things about her.

'Doing fine, and you?' If Holly wanted to play proper he'd play by her rules, this time. Amusement started creeping into his tone, however.

She frowned; it was now or never. She didn't think she wanted to answer the inquisition she was sure Emmie would give her if she didn't follow through. The worst he could do would be to say no. She'd say she understood and then hang up.

'Er—you mentioned if I changed my mind about the dance I should call you. I would like to go, if it's still all right?' She said it all in a rush. Too fast. Damn, why couldn't she be calm and collected like the society girls her uncle always wanted her to emulate?

'That's very much all right. I'm glad you can make it. I'll pick you up around seven.'

'OK.' She almost sagged with relief. He hadn't laughed at her. And he still wanted to take her. She smiled as a small bud of happiness blossomed within her. Suddenly she didn't want to hang up, didn't want to end the tenuous tie they'd established, but she couldn't think of anything else to say either. She wasn't usually tongue-tied like this. She could discuss cattle and horses and ranching and racing with the best of them. What was it about this man that made her so self-conscious, so nervous, so unsure of herself?

'See you then, Doc.' There was definite amusement in the tone now.

Holly nodded, then realised he couldn't see her. 'Sure, goodbye.' She hung up slowly, a stupid grin on her face. She was going to the dance and with Cache McKendrick, a man who usually didn't even take anyone to town affairs. Since Trish.

Who was Trish?

The dance didn't mean anything; it was only because she needed to meet people that she was going. Find a few friends she could do things with during the next few months. She didn't want to become too entrenched here. This was a temporary assignment, and she'd do well to remember it. Dr Watson would be returning in less than six months and Holly would be moving on. Back to

Kentucky, at last ready to face her family and demand her place at Windmere Farms.

Holly schooled her features and went to let Emmie know what happened.

'Well?' that woman asked as Holly joined her in the reception area of the small office.

'He'll take me,' she said in an offhand manner. Even as she said it, Holly felt a warm spurt of anticipation. When she met Emmie's eyes, it was all she could do to keep the silly grin from her face. She would meet other people who lived near by, expand her group of friends and feel as if she belonged a little bit. For a little while. And get to spend the evening with Cache McKendrick.

'Good. Fine man, Cache McKendrick. You know we're out of liniment?'

Holly blinked at the change of topic. 'And?' Was that critical?

'Usually Doc Watson kept some on hand, so he'd have it if that was all that was needed when he got called out. He usually got it over at Frank's Feed and Grain, on the far side of town.'

'OK. I'll stop in tomorrow and pick some up. Did Dr Watson have a preferred brand?'

'Don't know about that. Just get what you think is good.'

The next afternoon, after visiting a small homestead with three horses that only needed to be tube wormed, Holly followed Emmie's directions and drove over to Frank's Feed and Grain. Parking the jeep in the shade of one of the trees near the Feed and Grain, she wandered inside. She could see a man working in the barn section that opened off from the store part, but she continued walking to the aisles carrying animal sundries. She'd get what she needed and then have him ring it up.

She scanned the items, a slow smile starting. Brand names that were as familiar to her as toothpaste leaped out. She smiled, as if recognising old friends. So many of the different brands of liniment, neat's-foot oil and saddle soap were brands her uncle had used when she had been growing up at Windmere Farms.

There, near the bottom, Old Tom's Brew. She knelt down to take one of the bottles and read the label. It brought back such memories—working with the grooms on the horses, mucking out stalls for the privilege of riding Blue Boy. Trying it out on her own ankle when she'd fallen that time. God, she missed home!

'Howdy, Cache, how are you?' the booming voice of the proprietor called across the store.

Holly froze, clutching the bottle of liniment, memories vanishing instantly. Listening to hear if it was Cache McKendrick. Though how many men named Cache would there be in a town the size of Waxco?

'Howdy, Frank. Came to pick up some of that grain you and I discussed.'

She'd recognise that low, lazy voice anywhere; it was Cache. Holly could hear them clearly, though they were probably two or three rows away, where the store part opened out to the barn where Frank had bales of hay, both alfalfa and red oat stacked alongside barrels and sacks of grain. She stayed where she was, the liniment bottle forgotten as she listened.

'I put a dozen sacks aside for you. Thought one of the boys might come to pick it up. You in town for long?'

'No, just came to get that. Wanted a break from paperwork. That'll be what drives me out of ranching one day, the blasted paperwork.'

Frank chuckled. 'That'll be the day, not after all you've done on your place. Want to back in your truck? I'll load it up.' Just then the phone rang. Holly heard Frank hurry to answer it. Where was Cache? Going to get his truck? She debated standing, seeing if he was around. She could at least speak to him. Her heart sped up at the thought. Too much; maybe it would be better if she didn't see him. He'd be by to pick her up for the dance at seven tomorrow. She didn't need to see him before.

'Well, if it isn't Cache McKendrick. I haven't seen you in ages.' The purely feminine voice Holly heard wasn't Frank. She stood up; could she see the speaker? The shelves were too high; she couldn't see anyone. She stood still a moment, debating whether to walk around the end and see Cache and the newcomer, or remain where she was.

'Hello, sugar. I've been around, where've you been? Hello, Joe.'

'Cache. Brought this minx in to help me with some shopping. Heard Sunlight foaled. Doing OK?'

'Yeah. Came early, though.'

'Had the new vet?'

'Yes.'

Holly stood still, holding the bottle. She would not make her presence known now, though she would die if she was caught eavesdroping. Still, she didn't move, ears straining to hear better.

'What's she like?' Joe asked.

'Seems competent,' Cache replied.

Holly frowned; was that all he was going to say?

'I don't care about that. What I want to know is if you're going to the dance tomorrow, Cache.' It was the woman's voice again. Holly wondered what she looked like and who she was.

'Sure, sugar, aren't you? Save me a dance.'

'You can have every one, if you want.'

'And have every man in the county after me? No, thanks. One will do me.'

'Didn't think you'd let something like that scare you off.' Her voice was definitely flirtatious. Holly strained to hear what his response would be.

He chuckled. 'She's dangerous, Joe, you'd better watch her.'

'I know. If I can get her married off I'd be a happy man.'

'Dad!'

Holly wondered if 'sugar' and her dad would like her to marry Cache. She frowned. She hadn't even seen the woman, but she didn't like the idea of Cache marrying her.

'Come on, Sally, Frank's hanging up now and I want to catch him before he starts doing something else. See ya, Cache.'

'I'll save you a slow one tomorrow night, Cache...' The woman's voice trailed off as Holly heard them walking across the wooden floor, their footsteps fading as they walked. She replaced the old liniment, and picked up a bottle of the kind she normally used. She'd wait a moment, slip out to buy it, and be on her way. No need for anyone to know she'd been there.

Anyone meaning Cache McKendrick, of course.

'Hello, darlin'.' Cache came around the side of the aisle, and stopped when he saw Holly, his eyebrows raised in surprise.

She glanced up, startled to see him. Did he realise she'd heard their conversation? What would he think?

'Hi.' She looked back down at the bottle she held in her left hand, the fingers of her right hand rubbing against the label. Did he know she'd heard them discussing her? Couldn't he have said something more than 'seems competent'? She tried desperately for something to say, but nothing came to mind. Why couldn't she casually discuss the weather, or the mare and foal, and be on her way?

'You're going to wear off the label if you keep doing that.' His hand came out to cover hers, pulling it away from the bottle. It was warm, strong, firm, yet tender as he held her fingers.

She almost dropped the bottle. She didn't know the touch of a man's hand on her own could be so erotic. She felt his touch through to her toes, and her heart began a heavy beating in her breast. She chanced another look at him and found his eyes on her, the corners of his mouth turned up in a lop-sided smile.

Holly could scarcely breathe. She felt confined; the store was no longer big and spacious but small, crowded and stifling. Or was it just because he took up so much space?

Yet he didn't. He was just more blatantly masculine than anyone Holly had ever met before. It was overwhelming, menacing somehow. She was very conscious of her own femininity and she didn't like it. She wanted to be independent, on her own, able to hold her own in any situation. Not wondering if some man found her attractive. Not longing for him to do so.

His thumb began tracing lazy circles on the back of her hand. Holly could feel the touch throughout her whole body. She seemed in tune with the motion, yearning for more. She tried experimentally to pull her hand free, but he refused to release her.

'Don't let me keep you,' she said. The sooner he left, the sooner she could.

'You should have come and been introduced. Though you'll meet Joe and Sally at the dance.' His mocking tone told her he realised she'd heard every word. She looked away, trying again to pull her hand away. Wanting to put distance from this man. He could read her mind!

'You need to buy that from Frank; I can at least introduce you to him,' Cache said, glancing at the bottle gripped in her left hand.

'I may want a few more things.' She was not going over there now, with everyone still there. Nor was she going to cross this store with her hand in Cache's.

'Could you let me go?' she asked politely, her gaze on his chin. She was afraid to meet him eye to eye.

'Sure thing, darlin', for now.'

She sighed as he let her hand go. 'I thought I told you...'

'You're always telling something. Tell me what you're going to wear tomorrow night.'

She frowned, considering. She didn't have too many dresses. Jeans were the most suitable to her work. Since she didn't date much, she didn't have much need for a lot of party clothes. She darted a quick glance at his eyes, looked away. Suddenly she wanted to look nice for him on Saturday.

'I have a nice blue dress I could wear,' she said finally. 'I don't have a lot of clothes. How dressy is this dance?'

'I thought all women had lots of clothes. Why don't you?' He shoved his hat back on his face, his eyes watching her as she shifted nervously before him.

'Don't go out much. You didn't tell me how dressy the dance is.' It was not any of his business how often she went out.

He smiled at her, his eyes drifting down the front of her blouse, back to meet her eyes, sparkling as her anger built. How dared he peruse her as if she were some prime horse he was considering purchasing?

'Dressy for here, not dressy for a big city. Why don't you go out much?' He loved watching her flare up. Her eyes flashed sparks, he was sure of it. She stood so straight, as if trying to stretch out her brief inches. He smiled down at her as she searched for something scathing to say to him, anticipation building as he awaited her words.

'You sure are nosy,' she muttered, turning to walk towards the office, wishing she could think of something clever to say to wipe that amusement from his eyes. Maybe agreeing to go with him had been a mistake. Maybe she should change her mind again. No, he'd never let her forget that.

'You're being downright un-neighbourly, darlin'.' His hand was gentle on her arm as he stepped in front of her, his other hand going to her chin, cupping it with his warm fingers.

Holly paused, and for one shattering moment thought he would kiss her again. For one shattering moment longed for him to do just that. She held her breath.

'Cache?' Frank's voice called from the office.

'We'll pick this up later,' Cache promised, tapping her lips with his finger. Then he moved to wave to his friend.

Holly stared after him as he walked away. She could still feel the tingling imprint of his hand along her jaw, the caress of his fingers along her cheek as he withdrew it. The suggestive touch of his finger against her lips. She stared after him for long minutes, waiting for her body to calm down.

He was dangerous. She'd do better to stay away from the man; he was more than she was used to, more than she could cope with. And he was only playing with her, toying with her because she was so transparent and easy to rile.

Could she become more sophisticated? More casual about dealing with men on a sexual level? Why didn't she know how to flirt and flatter and walk away heart-whole? That was what her uncle thought she should practise—the gentle art of flirtation, not veterinary medicine.

Scowling, she hurried to pay for the liniment and seek the safety of her jeep. She saw a blonde woman in the distance, with an older man. Sally and Joe? Obviously Cache was well liked by one other woman in town, and Holly had no difficulty believing he would be well liked and sought after by all of them.

Yet he never took anyone to the town events, if Emmie was to be believed. Why not? She'd forgotten to ask Emmie about Trish. Emmie had mentioned her once, but not said who she was. A former girlfriend of Cache's?

And what would they all think when he arrived with Holly in tow?

Although she looked once more, despite telling herself she wouldn't, she didn't see him as she drove off.

Saturday was not the leisurely day Holly had hoped for. She'd planned to get ready in plenty of time to greet Cache with all the serenity she could muster.

Instead, late in the afternoon, she went into surgery when one of the dogs at a ranch beyond the Lone Tree was brought in badly torn up by barbed wire.

'Got tangled in a forgotten roll, struggled to get out.' The young cowhand who brought in the dog was distraught. It was his dog, and Holly knew he was scared for him. There was blood all over the dog and the man. 'Can you save him, Doc?'

Many of the cuts were superficial, though there were a couple on his legs that were deep and serious. Holly spent over two hours operating, and cleaning the dog up. Emmie worked right alongside her.

'Didn't know you were an O.R. nurse as well,' Holly said as she scrubbed up.

'Never had any formal training; Doc Watson taught me all I know.'

'Should be more than enough,' Holly muttered, already examining the dog. The surgery was not particularly difficult, just tedious and long. When she was finished, she went to reassure the owner.

'He'll be fine in a few weeks,' she told the cowboy who had waited so patiently in her office while she operated. 'Some of the cuts were pretty deep, he's lost a lot of blood, but I think he'll do just fine.'

'Gosh, thanks, Doc. That ol' dog means a lot to me.' He looked so young. Holly wondered how old he was; was he old enough to be working?

'Then you shouldn't have left the barbed wire lying around,' Holly said, rubbing her back. She was tired, and a quick glance at her clock showed her she only had twenty minutes before Cache would arrive to pick her up.

'You're right, Doc. We took care of that bunch. But there's always wire all over the range. You just have to watch for it. Thanks a million, Doc. Can I see him?'

Holly smiled and nodded. As he hurried off to see his dog, she hastened to get ready.

She had had her shower and was just finishing her hair when Emmie knocked on her door and stuck her head in.

'Cache is here. And he looks grand. So do you.' She smiled at the picture Holly made, still in her robe, her hair clean and shining, pulled back from her face to cascade in waves to below her shoulders. She had applied her make-up, except for lipstick.

'OK, thanks. I'll be out in a minute.'

'I'll be off, then. See you at the hall. Have fun tonight.'

Holly nodded, trying to apply her lipstick. Her hands shook; she was nervous. Just on the other side of that door was the man who annoyed her more than any other. And excited her more as well.

She smeared the lipstick, wiped it off and tried again. Getting it right at last, she went to the wardrobe to get her dress.

The knock at her door stopped her. Before she could answer, it was opened and Cache stood in the doorway.

'You sure are slow.' He ran his eyes over her, noting how the robe fitted her slight frame, the deep V caused by the lapels, the dark valley of her breasts that the robe displayed. 'You need any help?' His voice was husky, seductive.

For once the amusement was missing from his eyes, and Holly found the dark blue glitter she saw far more disturbing. She stared back at him. He was dressed in a dark suit, a crisp white shirt and a silver and grey tie. He looked sophisticated, cosmopolitan, and downright sexy. She'd seen him in old tight jeans, with and without a shirt, and now this. She caught her breath. He was gorgeous.

What was he doing taking her out? He could have any woman in town eager to go with him.

She couldn't look away, just gazed back at him, mesmerised by the look in his dark blue eyes, mesmerised by the pull of attraction that threatened to overwhelm her. Aware of the deep bronze of his tan, the faint lines radiating from his eyes, the white of his teeth as he smiled at her, and the strong body beneath the suit.

Holly blinked and broke contact. She took a deep breath, disturbed by the look in Cache's eyes as his gaze dropped to the opening of her robe when she breathed in.

'I don't need any help, thank you,' she said breathlessly.

He nodded and smiled again, that teasing, arrogant smile that caused her heart to flutter, and warmth to spread in her stomach. Damn, he was the most attractive man she'd ever seen. And she suspected he knew it.

'Just wondered. Emmie said you'd be right out, and it was so long I thought I'd check, to make sure you were all right.'

She longed to reach down and pull her robe up tight around her neck, but forced herself to give the appearance of being in control. She wouldn't let him know how much he disturbed her for anything!

'I won't be but another five minutes.'

'I'll wait.' His eyes roamed over her once more, then he stepped back and closed the door.

Holly let her breath out in a whoosh, leaning against the wardrobe door for a moment. Then, afraid he'd come back if she wasn't out in five minutes, she flew to get dressed.

The light blue dress was sleeveless, with a deep V-neck, fitted bodice and flared skirt. It was shorter than dresses she normally wore, ending above her knees, but fancy enough for tonight's dance. She debated for a long moment, then put on her highest heels. Her feet might ache by the end of the night, but she wanted everything she could muster to help her cope with Cache McKendrick.

Holly grabbed a light coat in case the night turned cold, and hurried to the living-room. Cache was standing near the window, looking out. When he heard her, he turned and watched her as she walked across the room towards him. His face was shadowed, and a look almost of despair crossed it before the familiar teasing grin appeared.

It didn't make sense. Why would he have looked like that? she wondered, dismissing the idea from her head. It must be her imagination. Cache had no reason for despair.

'You're a very pretty lady, darlin'.' His voice was low and sincere.

She smiled and inclined her head, the warmth in her heart more than she'd ever experienced before. 'Thank you, kind sir. I don't suppose it would do any good to tell you again not to call me darling.'

'Nope. Unless you want me to call you *Dr Murphy*.'

Holly wrinkled her nose and shook her head. She laughed. 'I give up. Just don't call me doctor in that horrid tone.'

'Nobody tonight is going to believe you're a doctor, anyway. Not looking the way you do.'

'What's wrong with how I look?'

'Not a damn thing, but you sure don't look like Doc Watson.'

She turned away, a small bubble of happiness within her at his compliment.

'Just let me check my latest patient and I'll be ready to go.'

Cache went with her while she checked on the dog, and asked her what had happened. She explained briefly as she checked the sutures. Satisfied the patient would be fine for the next few hours, she let Cache usher her out.

Another surprise. Instead of the dirty pick-up truck she had expected, Cache had a late model Ford, top of the range. She hoped she hid her feelings, but wasn't sure she had when he settled her on the leather seat and reached over to fasten her seatbelt.

'Weren't expecting this, were you?' His breath caressed her cheek, and his hand was warm against her hip as he snapped the buckle in, leaving his hand against the seat to support himself. His other hand rested on the back of the seat, near her shoulder. Holly felt fenced in, protected. He turned to look at her, his face mere inches from hers.

'I was expecting the truck.' Her voice was so soft, she scarcely knew what she was saying. She wanted him to kiss her so badly it was all she could do to keep herself from leaning forward and touching her lips to his. He was only inches away; she could feel his breath mingling with her own. Her lips trembled slightly.

'You leap to a lot of conclusions, it seems,' he said.

'Do I?' The seconds dragged by, slowly, slowly. Holly watched Cache, watched as his eyes stared into hers, as they moved lower to touch her lips, trace down her throat to the dark shadow showing in the V of her dress. Holly's heart pounded in her chest and her breasts felt heavy, tingling with desire. She watched as Cache's tongue darted out to lick his lips. She mimicked the movement, slowly licking her own dry lips.

His eyes caught the gesture and he stared at her moist mouth for endless moments.

Holly thought she would scream with the tension, throw herself against him and kiss him until dawn. When he looked into her eyes, she knew he saw how she felt.

'God, Holly, stop looking like that or we won't make the dance.' His voice was low, almost a growl.

She tried to drag her eyes away, but couldn't. She could only stare into the pools of blue that stared back at her. Lost to time, place and motion. Lost in Cache McKendrick's eyes.

CHAPTER FOUR

HOLLY dragged her gaze from Cache's and looked down at her hands lying loosely in her lap. Her heart was pounding so hard she was sure he heard it. She felt the butterfly caress of his breath as he sighed and ducked his head out of the car before standing up. He closed her door then rounded the car to climb into the driver's seat.

'It won't take long to get to the Grange Hall. That's where the dance is.' He started the engine and backed from her drive, glancing at her downbent head, his lips tight.

'Is this a special dance, or are there dances all the time?' she asked, conscious of his nearness. His shoulder was almost brushing hers, the seat back to its furthest notch to accommodate his long legs. Holly felt deliciously feminine near him. She was glad that the dress fitted her so well, that the skirt was short enough to show off her legs. Tonight she didn't want to be the vet, she wanted to be the girl Cache was taking to the dance, and bringing home later.

'Don't know about special. Twice a year the Grange puts one on, once in summer, and then at Christmas.'

Holly looked up and out of the window. She'd be gone by Christmas.

'Tell me a little about yourself, darlin'. I know you're not from around here, nor even California, not with that southern accent. Where are you from?'

'Kentucky,' she said softly, suddenly homesick for the gently rolling hills that would be green with the blue grass now. The white fences separating the pastures and paddocks of the horse farms that abounded in the area would be freshly painted. The old oaks would shade the pastures, flutter gently in the evening breeze.

Nothing in Kentucky was like the endless open sky here in California, the rolling grasslands that were already bleached by the hot summer sun, the hazy granite mountains rimming the valley in the far distance. This land was big and bold. She slid a quick peek at Cache; he matched the land.

'You're a long ways from home,' he commented as he passed the false fronts on the stores on Waxco's main street, light spilling out from display windows, one or two still open.

'I came to California to do my vet training.'

'Decided to stay?'

'No, I'm going back after this assignment.'

Cache flicked a glance at her, a strange stab in his heart. He'd just met her, and she was leaving? 'For a visit, or to stay?'

'To stay,' Holly said firmly, hoping in her heart that that was true. After all this time, she wanted to be able to stay at Windmere as the resident vet. Surely her uncle would at least listen to her proposal. Give her a chance.

'Doc Watson's getting old; he might consider taking on an assistant, if you do the job right.'

'No, I wouldn't be interested. I'm going back to Kentucky.'

Cache turned into the gravelled car park before the large Grange Hall. The old wooden building was painted red, with a metallic roof rising in an arch over the high walls. The car park was crowded, cars, pick-up trucks and even a couple of horses tied up near the entryway. Cache found a spot and soon Holly was escorted up the shallow steps to the entrance of the old building.

Inside, the foyer was large, panelled in dark wood, with a cloakroom to the right. Cache turned her there, took her coat and hung it up for her. For the moment they were alone, but Holly could hear the music, the murmur of voices, laughter. She took a deep breath, ready to meet the people of Waxco.

Cache stopped her in the doorway to the cloakroom, leaning over a little so that his face was close to hers. His hand caught her chin and tilted her face for his regard.

'I want you to have a good time tonight. I'll introduce you to as many people as I can. But remember who brought you and who's planning to take you home.'

She looked up at him and smiled. Was he unsure of himself? She doubted it. He was too confident, too self-sufficient.

'I'll remember,' she promised.

He rubbed his thumb gently over her lips, his eyes following the movement, then caught her gaze again. Holly felt her legs began to liquefy, and wondered if she sank into a puddle would he sink down with her?

'Good.' His voice was low, caressing, sexy.

The door burst open and two teenage girls came giggling into the foyer, pausing only a moment when they saw Cache and Holly.

'Hi, Cache,' one said, then giggled with her friend as they continued out through the front door.

Cache took Holly's elbow and escorted her into the large Grange Hall. It had been decorated for the dance with balloons and streamers and flowers. Tables lined the side-walls, some occupied, others still vacant, each covered with a snowy white cloth, a candle burning in the centre. It was festive and pretty and for the evening the austerity of the hall was forgotten.

At the far end was a small band, on either side of the entry door tables were laden with food and beverages. In the middle of the room couples were already dancing, others greeting friends.

'I like this song—come on.' Cache took her hand and led her to the centre, swinging Holly around and beginning to move to the music.

'Texas Two-step—you know it?' he asked as he guided her into the dance.

'I've heard of it.' She was trying to follow him, watching others, listening to the music. Holly liked all kinds of music, and wondered only fleetingly if tonight's fare would be entirely country-and-western. She followed Cache's lead, watched the others dancing and in only a few moments felt comfortable and relaxed, determined to enjoy the evening.

As soon as the music ended, they were surrounded by people wanting to meet Holly.

'This here the new vet?' an older man asked. His moustache was grey, his eyes grey, and his suit grey.

'Sure is; Holly Murphy, meet Doc Bellingham. He's the people doc,' Cache said as they shook hands.

'Us doctors have to stick together, right?' The older man smiled at Holly. When the music started he asked her to dance. With a brief glance at Cache, Holly agreed. Cache smiled at her and moved away, finding another woman to dance with.

The evening passed quickly for Holly. She met ranchers, shopkeepers and teachers. The wives were friendly, the men flirtatious, and everyone seemed to be there to have a good time.

Holly felt right at home and not at all out of place. She found the music changed from western to rock, then to slow, dreamy songs. Never lacking for partners, she danced almost every dance. Once or twice she caught sight of Cache, dancing with a different woman each time.

As the evening grew old, Holly wondered if she dared ask her next partner to sit the dance out. She was hot and thirsty and would love to sit on the side and drink a cool lemonade. And, as she'd known, her feet were hurting her. She smiled at her partner at the end of the song and turned to find a chair.

'My turn again, I think.' As the music drifted into a slow, romantic song, Cache caught her around the waist and turned her to face him.

Holly's fatigue miraculously vanished. Her body swayed towards his and she lifted her arms to encircle his neck without a word of protest. His own hands pulled her against him as the lights in the hall dimmed slightly. Her breasts pressed against the hard muscles of his chest, her legs moved in and out between his as they danced and turned and swayed with the music.

Cache lowered his head, resting his cheek against hers, and Holly closed her eyes, drifting along with the music, charmed by the man who held her in his arms. She forgot her thirst and being tired and hurt feet. She reached out to trail her fingers through the thick hair at the base of his head, wanting the moment to go on forever. Though Cache was tall, he accommodated his steps to hers, his cheek was warm against hers, his hands firm and caressing as they rested against her spine. Time stood still; there was only the two of them alone in a cloud of pleasure, swaying and dancing to the soft romantic strains.

'Mmm, nice,' Cache said softly in her ear, his fingers moving against her, traces of icy heat streaking down her spine. She shivered a little, and felt the heat of his fingers against her bare skin, stroking her, smoothing over her satiny skin, his touch gentle yet erotic in the crowded room.

Holly felt her defences slip away as she enjoyed the tactile sensations Cache evoked. His hands, his chest, the strength of his body, his slightly roughen cheek against hers. She sighed; it was wonderful.

The song ended and the lights came up. Holly stepped back and stared up at Cache, blinking a little in the sudden brightness. His eyes were dark as they gazed down at her, his hands still on her back, his fingers still tracking her spine. Her own hands hadn't left his neck, and it was difficult to bring them down.

Cache's lop-sided smile lit his face and he dropped his arms, taking her elbow in one hand. 'Come on, let's get something to eat and drink. The band's taking a break for a while and we'll take advantage of it.'

The food tables were crowded with others with the same idea, so Holly and Cache stood in line to get something to eat. Talking with others as they waited, Holly was slowly starting to associate faces with names.

'Cache, I've been trying to find you all night.' A pretty blonde girl came up to them in line and stopped by Cache. She put her hand on his arm and left it there as she smiled prettily around at the others.

'You promised me a dance, remember?' she said with a smile, but Holly heard a slight edge to her tone. That voice was familiar.

'Sure did, sugar. Night's not over yet. Besides, you've been dancing every dance,' Cache answered easily, shifting back slightly.

She tossed her head, glad at least that he'd noticed. She looked at Holly, a challenge shining from her eyes.

'And you're the new vet, I hear?' the girl said, moving slightly closer to Cache.

'Holly Murphy, Sally Lambert. Sally, this is Doc Watson's locum,' Cache introduced them, his eyes moving from one to the other, the teasing lights in them clear.

'How do you do?' Holly asked, smiling politely at the younger girl. If looks could kill, she'd be dead. Sally didn't want anyone around Cache, that much was evident.

'I do just fine.' Sally turned back to Cache, her eyes dancing. 'I heard the funniest thing earlier; you and the doc came in together and everyone was saying you brought her.' She laughed softly, inviting Cache to share the joke.

His eyes twinkled down at her and then at Holly. 'They're right. I brought the doc and am going to be taking her home.'

Holly looked at him sharply. For a moment she thought he meant to take her to his home. And keep her for always. She met his grin and smiled back, afraid to look at Sally Lambert, afraid to see the look in that girl's eye.

'Well, I guess the joke's on me. I didn't think you ever brought anyone to these things.' Sally's voice was brittle, the smile plastered on, but Holly could see the sudden hurt in the girl's eyes.

'Haven't in a while. Took quite a woman to accomplish that. Right, darlin'?' Cache caught Holly's eye and taunted her.

Anger flashed again. Damn the man, couldn't he see that Sally had a crush on him? Didn't he care that he was hurting her feelings? And *why* wouldn't he stop calling her darling?

She longed to say something that would cut him down to size. She even opened her mouth, but nothing would come. Closing it, she looked away, away from him to Sally.

'Actually, he just brought me so I could meet some people in town. So they'd feel comfortable calling me if they need a vet.'

Sally let her hand slide from Cache's arm and nodded, that same smile plastered on her face. 'I see; well, see you around, Doc. Cache, I'm still counting on the dance.'

'I'll find you later,' he promised.

Holly didn't speak while they stood in line. She purposefully kept her eyes averted, scanning the room, studying the tables with all the food piled high. It was none of her business how Cache McKendrick ran his life, but he'd been rude to Sally. It was unexpected from what she knew of Cache.

Filling her plate and getting a large glass of punch, Holly followed Cache to a small table towards the back. It had seats for four, but was empty. Only moments before she'd been elated at the thought of being alone with him; now she wished for another couple to help pass the awkwardness she felt.

She sat and sipped her punch.

'OK, out with it. You think I was wrong with Sally, don't you?' Cache's voice was hard as he sat beside her, slamming down his plate, his food forgotten as he nailed her with his eyes. His lips were tight and a muscle twitched in his cheek.

Holly met his gaze, her own firm. It was the second time he'd seemed to read her mind. She wasn't used to it. But if he wanted a fight, she was the one to give it to him.

'I think you were hard on her, yes, almost rude,' Holly answered. 'She's crazy about you.'

'And has been for ages. What am I to do, be polite and have her fancy herself in love with me all her life? She's a child. I don't want anything to do with her, except as a neighbour. I've tried being friendly, but she just thinks that means more, a lot more. So tonight I came on a little strong. Either way I lose.' He looked away, his face expressionless.

Holly stared at him, trying to see it from his side. 'Maybe what you did wasn't so bad, only she looked so hurt.'

'It's time she grew up. I haven't brought a woman to anything like this in ages, so I bring you. Maybe she'll realise I had all the time in the world to bring her, if I was ever going to do that. I'm not. I'm not interested in Sally Lambert.' He paused for a long moment, then swung back to look at Holly. 'But I am interested in Holly Murphy.'

'Don't be. Cache, I'm only here for a few months, then I'm leaving. I have to go back to Kentucky.'

'Have to? Why? Someone there waiting for you?'

She dropped her gaze, toyed with her food and tried to find the words. 'Ever since I was a little girl, I've wanted to work at my uncle's farm. He raises and races thoroughbred horses. I…it's the whole reason I became a vet. I've trained, studied and now I'm ready to go home. It's been my dream for as long as I can remember. And now it's almost here. And nothing and nobody is going to get in the way of it.'

Cache stared at her for a moment, then sighed gently.

'Yeah, well, hold on to it, darlin'. Dreams can shatter so easily. I hope you get yours, Holly.' He sat back, his eyes still on her, sadness welling. He'd thought he'd found someone with whom he might take a chance. But even before he had that chance, she'd ended it, with her quiet voice and shared dream.

Hell, who was he kidding? He'd tried that route once, and it had ended in heartbreak and death. He was too old, too wary to try again.

Holly didn't know what had changed, but the sparkle and delight in the evening faded. She was tired, confused and lonely. She glanced up as another couple joined them at the table. Her time for talking privately with Cache was over.

As was the way in ranching communities, the talk soon centred on cattle, horses and crops. The couple who joined them were Betty and Martin Basner, an older couple who lived beyond the Lone Tree ranch. Martin and Cache discussed cattle and the branding that would be coming up soon. Betty gave Holly information about the limited shops in town and where the best value could be found, and the few things she missed that could only be bought in a large city, like Reno, or Sacramento.

'Do you ride?' Betty then asked.

'I used to, all the time. Haven't had a horse lately.' It was one thing Holly missed most about being away from home. She'd ridden since she was four. The best times of her teenage years had been the afternoons she had exercised some of her uncle's horses.

'I've got plenty; come out some time and give them some exercise,' Cache said easily, leaning back in his chair, his eyes a deep blue. He ought to let her go, but he was never one to do what he ought to. If it meant he'd see her some more, he'd have her ride every damn horse on the place.

'I'd like that.' Holly smiled, suddenly pleased. She didn't know he'd been listening. It would be wonderful to go riding again, but she didn't know when she'd get the time. Unless . . . maybe she'd just make the time.

The band returned and started up immediately. Martin pulled Betty to her feet and they were away. Cache stood more slowly, reaching down for Holly.

'One more now and then I want the last one.' He swept her into his arms and moved her to the dance-floor.

Holly felt awkward with the recent conversation ringing in her ears. He was interested in her and she'd told him she would be leaving. Now what?

'Relax, darlin', we both know the rules now and no one has to do anything they don't want to. Maybe we can make some beautiful memories to remember down over the years.'

He drew her in closer and smiled down into her eyes, his hand again tracing fiery patterns against the bare skin of her back, his arms strong, holding her tight against him. He knew all about memories to hold for all the years. And he wouldn't let himself get too involved with this lovely lady. She'd made it clear she wasn't for him. And he knew better anyway, didn't he, by now?

'I like only happy memories,' she said softly, giving in and leaning against him, knowing this night would be one of the happy ones. Would he want to see her again? Make other memories?

'Happy? Or exciting?' he murmured as he dipped his head to trace feathery kisses along the side of her face, resting his cheek against hers.

She smiled and gave herself up to the dance, not wanting to examine how she would answer, but her heart's increased rhythm suggested exciting would be better. And everything connected with this man was exciting.

Holly found herself looking for Cache as the evening drew to an end. She saw him dance once with Sally, a fast-moving dance, nothing slow for that young woman. She saw him dance with Betty and with Dr Bellingham's wife. Each time the band paused she wondered if it was to declare the final song.

All too soon it was announced. Magically Cache appeared, and swept her into his arms for the last time that night. His smile was cocky and brash, just like the first day she'd seen him, but his arrogant attitude didn't rankle the way it usually did; tonight she sparkled up to him, feeling daring and sassy and able to match him all the way.

The lights dimmed until Holly could scarcely see Cache, but she could feel him against her, feel the delight in her body as it responded to the touch of his along the length of hers. As if by long habit, her arms encircled his neck, her fingers threaded themselves into his thick hair, relishing the feel of it. Relishing the feel of his arms around her, the solid strength of his muscular body against her softness, the feeling of anticipation and reckless danger.

She was floating on air, moving to the slow tempo, lost in the delight of being with Cache, of almost being a part of him.

He did not speak, moving slowly, sensuously against her, keeping her where he wanted her. When Holly felt his lips on her cheek, then brushing her mouth, the dreamy feeling intensified, the floating and surrealistic mood lingered until she felt as if the two of them were alone in a sea of starlight.

'I'm having the most marvellous evening, I never want it to end,' she said so softly she could hardly hear her own voice.

'Is that an invitation for me to stay the night?' Cache's amused voice asked softly in her ear.

Holly jerked back in shock. 'No, it is not! I meant, this dancing is fun.' She stared up into his laughing face, trying to see him in the dark, furious that she'd voiced her thoughts aloud.

'Somehow I didn't think you meant it.' He twirled her around quickly twice, and then leaned over and kissed her lips again. 'Come on, let's leave now, before the crowd starts to move and we get caught in Waxco's bi-annual traffic jam.'

He threaded his fingers through hers and led her from the dance-floor, avoiding other couples, heading for the door.

In what seemed like only moments they were pulling up before Holly's house.

'Thank you,' she began primly, nervously clenching her hands beneath the draped coat.

'I'd say the pleasure is all mine, but I think you had a good time, too.'

'Oh, I did. I had a wonderful time.' She smiled up at him. It had been a great night.

'Glad you changed your mind, then?'

She gave him a mock-frown. 'You didn't have to throw that up at me. So I was wrong. I'm big enough to admit it.'

He stared at her for a moment, taking seriously the words she said. 'Yes, I think you are. I'm glad you came tonight, Holly. I'll walk you to your door.'

Holly watched as he rounded the front of the car. Should she invite him in? Or just say goodbye on the doorstep? What if he kissed her? Again? Her heart began pounding at the thought, and she shivered slightly.

'Cold?' he asked as he opened the door.

'Just a little.'

He held her coat for her to thrust her arms inside and then threw his arm around her shoulders and escorted her up to the front door.

The porch light was burning, as was one small lamp inside. Holly unlocked the door, still wondering whether to invite him in or not.

He turned her to face him, his arms coming round her, his face lowering to hers. His lips were warm and firm as they moved against her and then opened hers. His tongue teased, then boldly thrust in to plunder the sweet moistness of her mouth.

Holly could scarcely breathe as the explosion of delight and delicious feeling cascaded through her body. His hands held her head where he wanted it as he drank from her lips. Holly stood quietly, revelling in the touch of his mouth on hers, the enchantment his touch brought almost overwhelming in its excitement. He'd offered her happy memories, or exciting ones. She much preferred exciting.

When he lifted his head, Holly stared up at him, her mouth still parted, her heart racing, her breathing shallow and gasping. She didn't want him to stop. She'd never felt like this before and wanted it to continue.

'Come any time to the ranch; I'll always have a horse for you.'

She nodded, her head tilted for another kiss.

But, without another word, he turned and left.

Holly didn't move for long minutes after the red tail-lights of the car disappeared down the road. Then, slowly, as if awakening from a dream, she turned and went into the house, a smile still on her lips. The lips that still yearned for kisses from Cache McKendrick. For a moment, Kentucky seemed a long way off.

Three days later she decided she'd waited long enough. Dressing in jeans and pulling on her boots, Holly thought about it again. Three days after the invitation to use his horses was time to show she was interested in riding, but not throwing herself after him. She'd show up, and if he was there, fine; if not, surely he would have told one of his men it was OK if she rode one of his horses.

It wasn't as if she was going just to see him. She'd made that very clear at the dance. But she would like to ride again. It had been several years since she'd ridden regularly, though when working at the riding academy she had been able to snatch a ride now and then.

There was no one working on the fences alongside the dirt road when she turned in. Holly pulled all the way into the barnyard without seeing anyone. There were several pick-up trucks scattered around, but still no sign of a soul. She hadn't expected that. Surely there was someone around, someone who would hear her jeep and come to see who had arrived.

After waiting in the car for a few minutes, she climbed out and headed into the barn. If no one was around, she'd just check on the mare and foal, and be on her way. Next time she'd call first to let Cache know in advance that she was coming.

'Howdy, Doc.' Sam was sitting in the tack-room, braiding some leather, the door open into the barn.

'Hi, Sam. I thought the place was deserted. Cache said I could come riding some time. Is today good?'

'Sure thing. He told us to expect you, didn't know when, though. I'll get him.'

'Oh, there's no need. I can saddle a horse if you'll just let me know which one.' Holly was suddenly shy about seeing Cache.

Sam didn't say anything, just kept on walking out into the yard. He reached in the jeep and blew the horn several times. In only a moment Cache came out of his house, slamming his hat on his head. Right behind him was Sally Lambert.

'Oh, lord, what now?' Holly murmured from the wide double barn doors. She hadn't expected to see Cache, and especially hadn't counted on running into Sally Lambert again.

'Howdy, darlin', came to go riding?' Cache smiled at her as he drew near, his eyes running over her, approval evident when he met her eyes again.

'If it's convenient. Hello, Sally.'

'It's convenient,' Cache said shortly.

'Cache, I've come to call and you're going riding?' Sally asked, her angry glance turned to Holly.

'Sally, you've been here a half-hour. You said you wanted to see the foal, so go see him. Sam'll show you the way. Come on, Holly, I'll get a horse for you. How well can you ride?'

Holly was almost afraid to turn her back on Sally, so strong was the girl's anger. But she answered Cache's questions and in only a few moments he'd picked out a bay gelding for her. He chose a big western saddle and effortlessly swung it on to the horse.

'Most of your riding was probably English, coming from Kentucky,' he said as he tightened the cinch.

'Only till I came out here. Doesn't matter, I can ride anything.'

He grunted and slapped the stirrups down. Before she knew it, Holly was lifted and placed in the saddle. He put her foot into the stirrup and ran his hand along her leg to test for the right length.

It was all Holly could do to remain still when his warm palm moved up her leg, testing for the rub of the saddle, testing for tightness of fit.

'Cute foal; what did you name him?' Sally came back to the yard, Sam a few feet behind her.

Cache paused and turned to face her, his hand still resting against the inside of Holly's thigh, near her knee. She swallowed hard and looked at the horse's ears. She could feel Cache's hand like a brand imprinting itself against her for all time. Her stomach began a strange dance, her skin grew warm and all her being focused on his hand, now gently moving against her leg, driving her wild with its feel, with the caressing.

'Starlight, because he was born at night out of Sunlight.' Cache was hard pressed to ignore Holly, his hand gently moving against her leg, feeling the softness through her jeans. He looked at Sally, but felt only Holly.

Holly squirmed slightly in the saddle and leaned over the far side to slip her boot into that stirrup, trying surreptitiously to dislodge his disturbing hand. To no avail. Sitting up, she gathered the reins, sliding from side to side in the saddle.

Cache looked up, met her eyes, his own brimming with amusement. Slowly he moved his hand back down, trailing fire the whole way. Holly glared at him and backed the horse a few steps.

'Right. Everything's fine. Where should I ride?' She was glad her voice wasn't as breathless as she felt. She saw Sally look at her again, speculation rampant in her face. Maybe she didn't do as good a job of covering up how she felt after all.

CHAPTER FIVE

'WAIT just a minute and I'll get my horse. I'll show you the way out, point out some landmarks so you can find your way back. Next time you can get Beau yourself. Don't want you getting lost, though.'

Holly nodded, and started her horse walking a little, to feel his gait, and to avoid having to look at Sally, though she could still feel the angry girl's gaze.

'I want to come too, Cache,' Sally said, much as a child might when worried it would miss a treat.

But Cache had already entered the barn. Sally paused only a moment and then followed him in, determination stamped on her face.

Sam moved to lean against the fence, his face grinning. Holly threw him a glance, her own lips turning up in a smile.

'Little miss sure is hard-headed. Ain't no way Cache is interested in her. Don't know why she cain't see it.' He shook his head. 'But she's been hanging around for a long time. Maybe one day she'll realise the boss can pick and choose, and he ain't choosing her.'

'Which way, Sam? I'll just walk slow; Cache'll be able to catch up.' Holly glanced once at the barn, anxious to be on her way. She didn't want to see Sally again. And she didn't believe Cache would let her accompany them on the ride. That man knew what he wanted and nothing got in his way.

'Head to the right of the house; you'll see a trail that leads up that slight hill yonder. He'll catch you.'

She smiled, nodded, and started out. Skirting the house, she had a chance to study it. It was the same sandy colour of the ground, the roof a reddish-brown tile. The windows were large and the front ones overlooked the barn and corrals. As she passed, she saw the green back yard, with patio and flowers and trees. It was like an oasis in the dry desert, or in the high desert.

Slowly Beau took the hill, following the path as if he knew the way. Holly settled into the saddle and gave herself up to the enjoyment of the ride.

In only five minutes Cache, riding a big chestnut horse, caught up. He rode the horse as if it had been especially invented for him. His legs casually held the horse, his muscles corded beneath his snug jeans. He sat straight, effortlessly guiding the large horse, slowing as he caught up with Holly. Together they crested the hill, and drew in to gaze across the vast land spread before them.

'This is great, Cache, thank you.' Holly smiled as she stared at the endless range land that lay before her. To the left, small hills gently rolled off into the distance, the bleached grass dotted here and there by the dark green live oak trees. Before her the flat valley floor extended for miles, in the distance a strip of green suggested water. To the right she could glimpse the mountains, shimmering in the hot sun.

He pointed out a landmark of rocks and sage, so that she'd know how to find the ranch again. Then he led the way towards the belt of green.

'It's Ash Creek. Cuts through the land here, keeps on going till it dumps into the Spooner reservoir. Gets pretty low in the fall,' Cache called over his shoulder.

Holly nodded, her eyes watching him as he rode. His shoulders were broad, filling his cotton shirt, his hat pulled low on his head, shading his face from the hot afternoon sun. He was as comfortable on his mount as any of her cousins had ever been. Somehow the long stirrups and backward slant of the western saddle made him look casual, unconcerned. Not the same as the neat military precision her cousins demonstrated but somehow more a part of the horse.

Cache belonged to the western lands. And Holly's heart began a rapid beat as she continued to watch him. He was much more interesting than the ground she was riding over. Suddenly there were a million questions she wanted to ask him. Was he originally from Waxco? How did he own the Lone Tree? It was huge; had he inherited it? Bought it? Why wasn't he married? He was attractive, there was no denying that. Though his arrogant manner might grate on some women.

Holly blinked and looked away, towards the water, now visible as they drew closer. He was an arrogant cowboy, but so far she'd held her own against him. Could she always?

He drew up near the bank of the wide river. The water flowed sluggishly across the riverbed, shallow in spots, deep as the channel bent around some old cottonwoods. The air was slightly cooler by the water and Holly was glad to draw up and rest. It was hot in the sun.

'You should wear a hat next time. This sun's brutal,' Cache said.

'You're right.' Her voice was soft, agreeable. He was right, so it was no use standing on her pride for that.

He scowled as if he didn't like her answer, as if he'd been looking for a fight. With a lithe move, he dis-

mounted and walked to the water's edge. Pulling a blue
bandanna from his back pocket, he soaked it in the cool
river. Turning, he carried it to Holly.

'Here, wipe down your face, it'll cool you. Do your
neck, too.'

The bandanna was still dripping, and water was
running down his arm as he held it up to her. Holly took
it and touched her forehead. It was cold, but felt great.
She patted her face, her throat, the back of her neck,
the water dripping down on her shirt, on her arms,
cooling her wherever it touched.

Cache watched her as she moved, his head tilted back,
his hat still shading his eyes. Holly felt suddenly self-
conscious, and handed him back the blue cloth with a
shy smile.

'Thanks, that was great. I'll remember the hat next
time,' she said shyly.

He mounted and moved his horse slightly until he was
next to her, his leg brushing against her. Holly looked
at him, determined not to give way. What was he trying
to prove now?

'See that fence in the distance?' He leaned near her,
pointing out the area he wanted her to look. Holly could
feel his breath brush against her cheek as she tried to
find the fence. His arm was near her shoulder, his head
near to hers. If she turned her face, could she touch his?
She swallowed hard, trying to find the damned fence.
Her skin quivered in anticipation and desire for him to
touch it. Memory of the dance, of his warm hands on
the bare skin of her back flooded her mind and her eyes
focused on his hand pointing out the fence, and not the
object of his interest.

'That marks the northern pastures. I run Herefords there, several thousand head. Then swing around...' His arm moved in an arch and when Holly turned to follow it she was close to him. She took a deep breath and forced herself to look where he was pointing.

'There starts the southern pastures and I run Texas longhorns there.'

'I heard they were making a come-back. Doing all right?' The vet in her took over.

'Yep, have to watch them a little in the winter months, but so far they're flourishing. Mean bastards, though. The Herefords are much easier to deal with. But I'm building the longhorn herd now, only selling off the old ones until I have the size herd I want.'

'Diversity is good,' she murmured, looking back at the cool water of the river. Did he ever come swimming here? The banks beneath the cottonwoods were grassy, green and inviting. Maybe she'd bring her swimsuit some time and ride out here.

'Yes, plus the longhorns have leaner meat. That's the trend today, so I want to be part of it. But you stay away from those pastures on your rides. Those animals are not much better than wild buffalo, and I don't want to have to go hunting you some day.' He turned to look at her as he issued his order, his teasing air gone. He was in dead earnest.

'OK.' Nothing would spoil this day. She was riding again, and it felt good. The country was wide and open and free. She had plenty of places to explore without going towards the more rocky slopes where grazed the longhorns.

They followed the river for a couple of miles, talking casually about ranching, cattle and horses. Holly longed to ask him other questions, to learn more about him, but fear of his mocking tongue kept her quiet. He was too much on her mind, she decided. In the future, she'd try to come when he wasn't around. Though the rides would not be as much fun, a small voice whispered inside her.

When they reached the stables, no one else was in sight. Cache dismounted, and threw the reins over the top bar of the fence. He came around and reached up for Holly before she could dismount herself. His strong hands encircled her waist and he gently pulled her from the saddle, deliberately letting her body slide down the length of his, his eyes capturing hers, holding hers the whole time.

She caught her breath at his touch, at the erotic feel of her body gliding against his. Her hands caught his shoulders, to steady herself, but remained there, even when she was standing again, reluctant to move. She looked up to his face, but his expression was shuttered, closed. He stood silently in the sunlight, staring down at her.

'I'll help you put the horses away,' she said for something to break the tension that she felt growing between them.

He didn't speak, but nodded, his hands slowly releasing her, trailing delight as they caressed her waist before leaving. Slowly he raised his hands to cover hers still on his shoulders and brought them down, then laced his fingers through hers for a long moment. His hands were hard, callused and strong. Holly glanced at their linked fingers; his hand was so much darker; her own were still pale. She was puzzled; they should be fiery red with the heat she felt from his touch. The tingling ran up her arm, touched something deep within her.

'Come on, I'll show you where Beau is kept; you can get him any time,' Cache said, at last releasing her, stepping away to put distance between them.

Holly nodded and followed Cache into the barn. It took only a short time to unsaddle and brush down the horses. Giving him a final pat when she was finished, she checked the manger.

'No hay—shall I fill it?' she asked, slipping out of the half-door and moving over to the stall where Cache was still working.

'Up in the loft, we keep the hay stacked there. There should be some flakes already broken out.' He slapped the rump of the big gelding and moved out.

Holly climbed the ladder leading to the loft, and spotted the bale of hay that had been cut open, flakes already broken apart. As she walked that way, she heard Cache behind her.

It was hot in the loft, the heat from the sun beating through the roof, the heat from the barn rising to the pitch. The sweet smell of hay permeated the air. Holly wished she had Cache's wet, cool bandanna up here. A faint sheen of perspiration coated her brow and she was hot all over.

The loft was opened all along the centre of the barn. When Holly peered over the edge, she saw that the stalls were set up so that hay could be pitched directly into the mangers for the animals. It was a clever way to lay out the barn.

Reaching for a flake, she found Beau's stall, and judged the aim to the manger. Letting the flake drop from her hands, she smiled with satisfaction when it landed square in the manger. The horse ambled over and began munching.

Still smiling, she turned to watch Cache as he dropped hay into Roman's stall, and turned to look at her.

'It's hot,' he said, wiping an arm against his forehead and taking a step closer to Holly. Involuntarily, she stepped back, then again. Away from the edge of the loft, away from the dizzy feeling she got if Cache came too near.

'Take off your shirt, if you're hot,' she said, looking for the ladder.

'I will if you do.' Cache's voice was low, teasing, his eyes dancing with laughter. He took a step forward.

Holly watched with fascination as he stalked her. She stepped back, he stepped forward. She stepped again, came up against the pile of stacked bales of hay. He followed until he almost touched her. His eyes never left hers, but the laughter faded, to be replaced by something else.

Cache took off his hat and reached around Holly to put it on the stacked-up bales. He ran his other hand through the golden hair, darkened slightly by perspiration.

Daringly, Holly reached up one hand and ran her fingers through his hair. Cache closed his eyes at her touch, standing so near her, yet only her hand touched him.

He opened his eyes and looked at her for another long moment, then lowered his head to kiss her. His lips were hot and moist and quickly moved to open hers. His tongue plunged in to taste her, to tease and torment her. His lips moved against hers, forcing a response that flared in Holly like a white-hot fire.

She was burning up. The air was hot, his mouth was hot, the feel of him against her hand was hot. She thought she would be consumed by the heat. The hay prickled against her skin, through the thin cotton of her shirt as Cache leaned into her and forced her back. Her hands encircled his neck and pulled him to her as his body pressed against hers, inflaming her further. She was so hot.

Pulling back only slightly, Cache looked down at her smouldering gaze. He smiled slightly and moved back enough to make some space between them.

'Unbutton my shirt. I'm hot,' he said softly, his arms braced against the stack of hay, holding himself around her, but not touching anywhere. Yet the heat of his body encircled her, enveloped her.

Holly felt trapped, but it was a silken trap, one she didn't want to escape. Slowly, her eyes gazing deeply into his, she slid her hands down from his shoulders to the front of his shirt. Her fingers didn't tremble at all when slipping the buttons through the holes, one after the other, working her way down the front of him, tugging on his shirt to bring it up from his jeans.

When the shirt was undone, she tilted her head slightly and a small teasing smile lit her face. Slowly her hands moved up the hot skin of his stomach, feeling his muscles contract and jerk against her touch. Her smile widened as her hands moved slowly up, tracing the strong cords of his chest muscles, brushing lightly against his tight nipples, conscious of the harsh gasp he gave when she did so. Reaching his shoulders, she eased his shirt away, his arms coming down to his sides as she pushed the shirt from his body.

His arms came up again, entrapping her between him and the stack of hay. The hot air barely stirred, Holly's blood pounded through her veins, heating her as it coursed through her body. Exhilaration filled her as she stared bravely up at him, the heat intoxicating, the feel of his skin still lingering on her fingertips. Danger hovered in the air, but Holly ignored it. She smiled up at Cache.

'Now you,' he said softly, his eyes dark and stormy.

'Me?' she squeaked. Her skin grew rosy. 'I'm not all that hot,' she protested, her breathing becoming decidedly uneven.

'Liar,' he said softly, as if gentling a spooky horse. 'Now you.'

This time her fingers did tremble as Holly slowly started to unbutton her own shirt. She could feel her heart pounding, pounding so hard against her chest, she knew he had to see it. Yet his eyes only saw into hers. Only saw the warm brandy colour of her eyes staring up into his. Only saw the tinge of colour as it climbed into her cheeks, warming them, kissing them as Cache longed to do. As he would do as soon as she had her shirt off.

The seconds stretched out endlessly as she slipped her buttons through the holes; it wasn't as easy as his had been. Why was she doing this? She should be on her way home, not up in a warm, fragrant hayloft, playing dangerous games with an exciting, sexy cowboy.

Sexy. It described Cache. She was afraid to apply the word to him, for fear she'd never be able to resist him. Well, it didn't look as if she was resisting him now. And he was sexy as hell, his dark blue eyes showing how he longed for her, his muscular arms and chest hovering over her, able to crush her to him and make her forget everything, his seductive lips ready to plunder her mouth again, inflame her, carry her to the heights of ecstasy and delight.

She licked her lips and his eyes moved then, to follow the movement of her tongue. A soft groan was forced from his lips.

Holly shrugged out of her shirt, sliding it down her arms. Cache stopped its movement, trapping her arms alongside her, pulling her against him, his mouth reaching for hers, his arms binding her against him, drawing her tightly against the warm skin of his bare chest.

His kiss wreaked havoc with her thought process; Holly gave up all attempt to think rationally; she gave herself up to the pleasure of his mouth on hers, his hands kneading the soft skin of her back, the heat from his body pressed most intimately against hers. It was heavenly.

She struggled, trying to get her hands free, wanting to hold him, wanting to feel his skin under her fingers. But he kept her trapped by her shirt.

Feeling her move, Cache broke the kiss and looked down at her; keeping one hand on her back, holding the half-off shirt in place, he reached his other hand to slide off the strap of her bra, first one, then the other, pushing the offending scrap of material away from what he sought.

Holly trembled against the sensations he caused; she couldn't think, she could only feel. She pressed herself against him, feeling the heat of his skin directly on her, the strength of his hard chest wall against the softness of her breasts. She drank in the scent of the man, mingled with hay and horses.

'God, Holly, you are so beautiful,' Cache said against her mouth as he again claimed her lips.

She struggled again and he at last released her, to let her free her arms, and then encircle him.

When he left her mouth to trail short, sweet, hot kisses along her cheeks to her jaw, she sighed in pleasure. Then his mouth moved lower to trace her throat with his hot tongue, to trace a hot, fiery trail down the slopes of her breasts to the rosy peaks; Holly was filled with erotic fantasies as never before.

Cache sank down, pulling Holly with him. He leaned back until he was lying on the hard wooden floor, the pricks of the hay unnoticed as he brought her to lie on top of him. Holly reached for his mouth, the pleasure and delight he was bringing beyond anything she'd ever experienced before. It was heady, indecent and oh, so exciting. He had been right again: exciting memories were far better than sweet ones.

His hands caressed her back, down her spine to the edge of her jeans, over the soft flare of her hips to cup her soft bottom. She could feel the heat of him through the thick denim. Back up to her back, her shoulders. His mouth held hers captive, pleasuring, deriving pleasure.

Holly didn't know which was better—to receive his kiss or give back some measure of her delight when kissing him. She was so hot, and her mouth felt swollen with passion. Her fingers tingled with the feel of his skin as she traced every inch of his body she could reach: the strong muscles of his shoulders, his arms, his neck; the thickness of his hair, the roughness of his cheeks, the hardness of his jaw.

'Cache?'

Instantly they froze. For a long moment Holly didn't move a muscle, except for her pounding heart and her ragged breathing. She couldn't move. Slowly she raised her head, staring in shocked surprise at Cache.

'Boss? You in here?' It was Sam, somewhere in the barn.

'Yeah, Sam, up in the loft. What's up?' Cache's voice rumbled against her as she lay on his chest. Quickly she scooted off, to sit beside him, feeling bereft and cold. He sat up, watching the ladder. His lips were slightly swollen, and Holly rubbed her fingers lightly over hers. They were puffy from his kisses.

'Call from Miz Eton. She says it's important and I should find you.'

'Hell!' Cache rose with one smooth movement and reached for his hat. Slamming it on his head, he hunted around for his shirt. Picking it up, he glanced briefly at Holly, then shook off the hay clinging to the cotton of his shirt. Shrugging into it, he leaned over her and kissed her lightly on the lips.

'Duty calls. Shouldn't be too long,' he whispered and headed for the ladder.

Holly sat still as she heard the men talking as they walked away, towards the house. When she could no longer hear them, she slowly put on her clothes and dusted herself off. Her heart was still beating heavily, but her breathing was under control. Descending the ladder, she glanced at the house as she walked to the jeep. She didn't see Cache, and she was not going to wait.

Heat madness had probably caused that encounter in the loft, and she was not as hot now that she was outside in the moving air. Starting the jeep, she backed it around and headed for home. Glancing at herself in the rear-view mirror she saw that her lips were rosy and swollen from his kisses, and her heart sped up, remembering.

She felt raw and exposed after all the kissing and touching in the loft. She was here in a professional capacity, not to become involved with one of the local ranchers, no matter how sexy. She was only here for a few months, filling in for the regular vet, then she'd be going home.

She wanted to go back to Kentucky. It had been her dream for seven long years. The dream had been even longer, if she counted all the time as a child she had yearned to be the vet at Windmere. She would not let a few passionate kisses change all that. She would not!

Hot and sticky by the time she reached home, she hurried to the bathroom and had a brisk shower. Bits of hay tangled in her hair, and her back still itched from pressing against the wall of bales.

She stood beneath the water, enjoying the feeling as it cascaded over her body. Washing her hair, she gave a brief prayer that all the animals around town would stay well; she hoped she didn't have to go out anywhere else today. She wanted to dress in shorts and a sleeveless top and nothing else, and sit and do nothing the rest of the day.

When she was dressed, she wandered back to the office. The flashing light told her of the messages on her machine. For a moment she felt guilty; she should have listened first. What if there was an emergency?

She had her pager with her; there had been no emergency.

Pressing the button, she sat on the edge of the desk to listen. Emmie called to remind her she'd be late in the morning. Dr Bellingham called to invite her to dinner in two days. Mike Slatter called to ask the doc to arrange some time to come and check on his bull, he seemed listless. Probably because of the heat, Holly thought.

The last voice was Cache's.

'Darlin', forgot to ask if you can go with us when we check on the yearlings. Need to see if we have any more branding and castrating to do, and you can give them the inoculations. We'll be gone a couple of days. Stan over at Overvilla usually subs for Doc Watson. If you can't go, I'll get Stan and you can sub for him. Call me.'

Her heart beat against her ribs as she listened to the familiar voice. She smiled, remembering why he had forgotten to mention the trip. Dared she go with him? For a moment she let her imagination run riot, then pulled it in. It would not be just the two of them; he'd have cowboys around, horses, cattle. There was work to do; it was hardly a tryst.

She called Dr Bellingham to accept; Mike Slatter to set up an appointment in the morning; Stan Connors to see if he could sub; and lastly Cache, to agree to the cattle trip.

'We'll leave next Wednesday. Shouldn't be gone more than a week or so. You want me to call Stan?' He was all business.

Holly longed to ask what was so important with his call with Mrs Eton, and who she was to begin with. But she didn't know him well enough. If he wanted her to know at this juncture, he'd tell her. Besides, he hadn't mentioned the interruption, or what had been interrupted. She was too shy to do so.

'I've already called Stan. What do I bring?'

'Just jeans and some shirts. We'll have everything else. Thanks, Doc.'

Before she could even ask if he was talking about the Herefords or longhorns, he hung up. Holly stared at the phone for a long moment, then slowly replaced it. She'd have a reason to talk to him next time she went riding—find out more about this cattle drive, and what he expected of her.

Though maybe it would be better if she didn't go riding if Cache was around. She was afraid she would be thinking more about being with him than staying on some horse.

Holly stayed away from the Long Tree for three days. *That seems to be my limit,* she thought as she turned into the driveway in the early afternoon of the third day since she'd last seen Cache. She'd brought a cowboy hat to shade her face from the sun, and had on a clean shirt and jeans. Her glossy brown hair was pulled neatly back in a braid. She didn't plan to see Cache, but wanted to look nice just in case she ran into him.

The yard was as deserted as before when she drove up. She grabbed her hat and walked to the dim coolness of the lofty barn. Pausing a moment to let her eyes adjust after the bright sun, she checked on Sunlight and Starlight before going to get Beau, dozing in the stall. She called his name softly as she walked up to his stall, so as not to startle him.

He came awake and turned to thrust his muzzle against her open hand. Holly stroked him for a few minutes, the soft, velvety feel of it always a pleasure. She patted his neck and checked his hoofs, talking to him the entire time.

'Want to go for a ride, old fellow?' she crooned. One more quick glance around showed her she was alone. With an unexplained sigh, she found the saddle she'd used before and in only minutes she and the gelding were heading past the ranch house and out to the open pasture beyond.

She urged to horse to a lope and they thundered across the sage towards the river, the hot air streaming by, giving a momentary illusion of coolness. When they drew near the river, she turned towards the south, pulling Beau into a jog-trot and then finally into a walk.

'Don't want you getting too hot,' she said as she patted his damp neck. There were plenty of things to see and Holly didn't want to miss anything.

After an hour, she moved to bring the horse towards the landmark Cache had shown her before. They slowly picked their way through some rocks, the horse surefooted and steady on the uneven ground. Holly was hot and sweaty now, and feeling wilted. The hat kept her shaded from the sun, but she was still feeling the heat, and wished for some sort of breeze.

Near the top, she saw a small black ball of fur struggling near some rocks. She drew in the horse and studied the situation. It appeared that the small animal's paw was trapped by a cleft in a rock.

Holly couldn't ignore it, though she saw with a shock the white stripe down the back.

'Well, now what?' she said aloud. The horse's ears twitched, but he stood patiently, awaiting her signal to proceed. The little skunk mewed softly, scrambling against the rocks, trying to dislodge his paw. But he was tightly trapped.

'Damn,' Holly said as she dismounted.

CHAPTER SIX

HOLLY reined in near the house, looking at the men in the yard near the barn. It looked as if every cowboy on the blasted ranch was standing around. She thought bitterly about her other visits when she couldn't find a soul. Why not this time? She could see Cache leaning casually against her jeep, talking to one of the younger men. Three others were in the corral, lethargically lassoing the horses, releasing them. Just for practice, as far as she could tell. Two more were leaning against the rail fence, watching the ropers.

'Damn and blast,' she said again, breathing through her mouth, knowing there was no avoiding them. She just wanted to get home and wash and get rid of the smell of skunk. But she hated to have to announce it to the world. Maybe she'd bypass the house, gain the main road and ride Beau home, coming back after she'd showered.

Too late; someone must have seen her and told Cache. He turned and looked in her direction, pushed off from the jeep and started walking towards her. Holly bit her lip in indecision, watching him approach her, his step easy, his body moving with the smooth fluid motion of a wolf on the prowl, a panther hunting its prey. She shivered slightly as she watched him approach, feeling pinned by his gaze. She wished she could turn around and ride away.

Instead, she urged the horse forward slowly, moving as if in a trance towards the man.

Cache stopped a few feet from her, and she pulled Beau up.

'Whew, is that you?' he said, his face frowning at the stench.

She tilted her chin slightly and nodded crisply. 'I found a skunk caught in some rocks; I had to help him.'

'God, you're lucky Beau brought you home.' The corners of his mouth twitched as he reached out and grabbed the rein near the horse's mouth.

'Once we started going, I was downwind of him.' She dismounted, jumping a little the last few inches. She was not tall enough on this slope to reach the ground with a foot in the stirrup.

She eyed him warily. 'You want to bring my jeep here for me, and I won't have to share this with all your men?'

Cache grinned, shook his head. 'You don't want to be doing that, darlin'. You'll smell up your car. I'll take old Beau here back to the barn; one of the men can take care of him. You need a bath.'

'I'll get one at home.'

'And have skunk fragrance be your companion the rest of the summer?'

She frowned; she didn't want her jeep to smell like skunk. She was almost sick from it herself right now. She only wanted to wash it all off and never have to smell it again. Cache did make some sense.

'OK,' she agreed reluctantly.

'Did you help him?'

She smiled and nodded; that was the only thing that had gone right. 'Yes, he was trapped in some rocks, and I got him free. Fine thanks he gave me.' She laughed a little. She'd known he would probably spray her, but she couldn't let him stay trapped.

'Where did he get you?'

'All over, can't you tell?'

'Boots?'

'Maybe not. I hope not.' She looked at the boots, dusty and dry. How could she tell? She thought the spray had just hit her as she was turning away, trying to evade the little critter's shot.

'Wait here.' He led the horse back to the barn, speaking briefly with one of the cowboys. In only a moment, Holly could hear the laughter as the tale spread, saw the men turn to look her way.

'Wait until you have an embarrassing moment,' she muttered beneath her breath as he started back towards her. All sorts of scenarios flashed in her mind for getting even with him. But, she sighed, none would probably come true.

When he got near her, he veered around, motioning for her to follow him. Holly couldn't really blame him; she did smell awful. And she didn't want to get it on anything else.

At the back of the house, he stopped, and looked at her.

'I'll help you get your boots off. No sense in getting them wet.'

She eyed him suspiciously. 'What do you mean?'

He smiled. 'Now, darlin', how do you get rid of skunk?'

'Wash it off.'

'Nope, won't do it.'

'With soap?'

He shook his head. 'Need tomato juice.'

She looked startled. 'You're nuts.'

'No. Wait here.' He entered the house, leaving Holly standing in the dusty yard. She could not see the barn or any of the corrals from where she was. All she could see were the hills and the endless blue sky. And smell skunk.

Cache appeared with two large cans of tomato juice, and a cloth.

'You're joking, aren't you?' She eyed the cans of juice warily. She looked at him; he was smiling broadly.

'No. Sit down so we can get your boots off.'

He waited until she sat on the steps, then put down the juice and cloth and reached to pull off her boots. He placed them near the door.

'The acid in the tomato cuts through the skunk oil; only thing I know about that cuts it clear through so you can wash it off. Otherwise the smell will linger for days.'

'Yuck, the cure is almost as bad as the ailment,' she said in distaste. She didn't want to bathe in tomato juice.

'Strip off your clothes.'

'What did you say?' She eyes flew to his in shock.

Cache looked up at her, his eyes dancing; he pushed his hat back on his head the better to see her. 'Take off your clothes. They probably got the worst of the spray. I'll find something for you to wear home. These should be burned.'

'I am not going to strip down for you or anyone...' she began hotly.

He laughed and leaned near her, careful to avoid touching her.

'Darlin', you will never be safer. You stink to high heaven right now, and soon you will look and smell like a tomato. You are as safe as you'll ever be.'

Holly didn't like him laughing at her, but as she stared back at him she realised the truth of what he said. Not that she liked it. And she would not strip down before him!

'I can do this myself. I'll pour the juice on me in the tub.'

'I don't want my plumbing backed up. Tomato juice stays outside.' He stood beside her, tall, his legs spread, immovable.

'Then I can manage by myself; just leave the juice.'

'How are you going to get your back? Your hair? Come on, darlin', stop arguing and get going. You smell awful.'

'Don't keep saying that!' she snapped, unbuttoning her shirt, remembering inadvertently the last time she'd unbuttoned it before this man.

She wished she had worn a serviceable cotton exercise bra, instead of the frilly bit of lace and cotton she had on. But he'd seen more the other day in the loft. And she knew he was right: she wasn't tempting today. She wrinkled her nose; she did smell awful.

At least her briefs were of serviceable cotton. She stepped out of her jeans and pulled off her crew socks. Actually her bikini revealed more than her underwear. But telling herself that didn't help. She still felt more exposed, more vulnerable before him.

Cache watched her, his eyes twinkling. He rose and moved near her, one opened tomato juice can in his hand.

'I wear cotton briefs too,' he said softly, and leaned over to touch her lips lightly with his.

Holly licked her lips when he pulled back, for a second forgetting the reason they were here, wanting more, wanting a kiss like the ones in the barn.

He paused, still close to her, and she smiled saucily up at him.

'If I throw my arms around you, I could share some of this delightful fragrance.'

'Then I'd have to share your shower with you,' he said, his voice low and seductive.

Holly stared into his eyes, seeing the growing awareness and hunger there. Knowing it must be reflected in her own gaze. She swallowed and looked away, but the hunger didn't fade.

'Pour on the juice,' she said, looking firmly at the hills.

Cache's touch was impersonal as he covered her with tomato juice, making sure all traces of the awful smell were neutralised. Holly practised thinking of other things as the cool, thick liquid dribbled over her. When she was coated to his satisfaction, he stepped back and tilted his head, looking at her.

She flashed around at him, raising a fist in mock-threat. 'If you say one single word, I'll deck you,' she said, her eyes sparking fire. But already the smell had faded. Maybe he'd been right. Not that she needed to tell him. He already thought he knew it all.

'I wouldn't dare,' he murmured, and reached for the hose.

'Don't...' She tried to move away but the blast of cold water caught her. 'It's freezing,' she shrieked, dashing to one side, trying to move away.

'Hold still.' He clamped one hand on her arm, dousing her with the cold water. 'You can't rinse this off in the shower.'

She grabbed the hose and turned it on him, smiling gleefully at his shout of surprise.

'Maybe not, but at least you know how cold it is.' She danced away, out of reach. Skimming the water off her, she wrung out her hair. 'I'm clean enough. Where's the shower?' She needed the privacy of his bathroom. The cold water had hardened her nipples; they showed taut and thrusting in the lacy bra. Her pants were almost transparent, offering no protection for a roving male eye.

And Cache's eyes were roving, all over her. Holly caught her breath; her skin tingled as if he were caressing her with his hands, not just his eyes. She stood transfixed, watching him look at her. Wishing he'd do more than just look.

'Stop that! Cache, where's your bathroom?' she asked again, shivering a little in the hot afternoon sun. She licked suddenly dry lips and took a step closer to the door. She needed to get away from him, away from the thoughts that were spinning in her mind.

His eyes narrowed and pierced hers. He started towards her, never looking away. Walking slowly with a hunting instinct.

Holly swallowed again, broke eye contact and scurried across the few feet of dirt to the back door, throwing it open to enter his kitchen. She paused for a moment, not knowing which way to go.

'This way.' His voice was calm, expressionless. He led the way down a hall, entering a large bedroom at the back of the house. 'Through there.' He pointed out the adjoining bathroom.

Holly hurried into the room and in only seconds was in the shower, relishing the hot water sluicing over her, quickly soaping up to get the stickiness of the tomato juice and the last traces of skunk off her skin. She washed her hair with Cache's shampoo, its spicy tang reminding her of him. Of the night of the dance, and the afternoon in the loft. Shaking her head at where her thoughts were going, she stayed beneath the spray until the water turned cool.

She dried off quickly, wrapping her hair in one towel, and wrapping her body in another one. She glanced at the sodden underwear on the floor, and wrinkled her nose. She didn't even want to touch it. But what was she going to wear home? She couldn't drive home through town wearing only a towel.

'Doc?' Cache called through the door.

'What?'

'I've left a couple of things for you on the bed. I know they'll be large on you, but you should manage to keep them on until you get home. I'll be in the living-room, back down the hall and to your right.'

She heard the bedroom door close and slowly she opened the connecting door from the bath. His room was empty.

The large king-size bed dominated the room, windows flanking it framing the view of the back of the house. Carpet on the floor muffled her steps as she walked towards the bed. She saw the cut-offs and sweatshirt laid out. Glancing once at the closed hall door, she quickly pulled up the shorts. They were a little loose on her, but wouldn't fall off. She pulled on the sweatshirt. It was huge. Patiently she rolled back the sleeves until her hands were clear. If she only had a belt, she could wear it as a dress.

Cache had left a large plastic bag as well, for her underwear, she assumed. She tidied the bathroom, using one of his combs to attack the tangles in her hair. Finally feeling refreshed and ready, she sought the living-room.

He was standing by the window, overlooking the front yard and out to the barn. This room was also large, airy and comfortable. It looked lived-in. Holly glanced around, seeing what she could learn about Cache by studying how he lived. The browns and golds of the room brought in the outdoors. The comfortable furniture showed her a man who liked comfort above show. Pictures on the walls were primarily outdoor, western themes. Several books were scattered around, a couple of magazines on the table. She couldn't read the titles, but the cattle on the cover gave her a clue to the material inside.

He heard her and turned. 'Better?'

'Much! Thanks.'

She wanted to go home, put distance between herself and Cache, between herself and what happened every time the two of them were together. Yet part of her wanted to stay, spend some more time with this unsettling man.

'I brought the jeep up, and put your boots in.' Cache moved slowly across the room, his eyes never leaving hers.

Holly took a deep breath. 'Thanks, I'll be going, then.'

'Come again, and we can go riding.' He stopped near her, but didn't touch her.

Holly wished he would.

'Yes. I'll bring your clothes back tomorrow.'

'I'll burn yours.'

She nodded, with only a twinge of regret for the new shirt. She didn't want those clothes back.

'You look like a little girl, playing dress-up,' he said, his eyes drifting down over the straight hair hanging down her back, the baggy sweatshirt, the shorts that hung to her knees.

'Better than going home in nothing,' she retorted.

'Definitely better to stay in nothing.' His voice was low, husky, his eyes met hers again and she could read the invitation, loud and clear.

'I'm going back to Kentucky,' she said desperately, as if that were a mantra that could protect her. Protect her from her feelings, which threatened to get out of control with this man.

'I know, but not today, not tomorrow. We would have that.' His voice was soft, seductive, sexy.

'I don't want that.' She backed towards the door. She was not one to go for one-night stands. If she fell in love, she'd want constancy, permanence, marriage. She was pretty sure those traits weren't high on Cache's list right now.

'Memories for the future.' His voice was enticing.

'No!' Holly whirled and hurried out of the door, the screen slamming behind her. Running from him, running from her own desire to give in to his suggestions and stay.

She lightly stepped across the short distance to her jeep, her bare feet not feeling the rocks and dirt, her heart thumping in her chest. Starting her car, she pulled away, her breathing erratic, and the desire to stay so strong it was almost overwhelming.

She saw Cache standing in the doorway watching her as she glanced in the mirror. For a moment she faltered, then with determination looked forward and carefully drove from his ranch.

She was going back to Kentucky. She didn't have time to get involved with some sexy cowboy whose eyes melted her insides, whose touch inflamed her senses and whose presence filled her with delight.

He was wild and carefree and not for the likes of her. Let him chase after the girls in town, and leave her alone. No more flirting with danger; Holly put temptation behind her as the ranch was left behind.

She reached home without incident and was soon dressed in shorts and a vest-top. The day was warm and the heat would linger far into the night. It was muggy and still and Holly wished for the first time that the house she was staying in had air-conditioning.

Sitting near a window, for what little breeze might stir, she picked up a book and tried to read. The stillness was oppressive and she had no energy. Slowly she let her eyelids close and dozed off.

The shrill ring of the phone startled her awake. Holly blinked slowly and looked around, for a moment disorientated to where she was. It was almost dusk; she'd been asleep for a couple of hours.

'Hello?'

'Doc? It's Sam. Sunlight's in a bad way. She took a fall. Don't know if anything can be done. Can you come to see her?'

'Sam, what is it? What's wrong?' Already Holly was thinking of what she needed to get, how long it would take her to get back to the Lone Tree ranch.

'She's down, Doc. Leg broken, maybe more. She's bad, Doc.'

'I'll be there as fast as I can drive.' Holly slammed down the receiver and raced to grab her bag and some antibiotics. She thrust her feet into tennis shoes and hurried out to the jeep.

Surprised she wasn't stopped for reckless driving or speeding, in only a few minutes Holly turned into the long driveway leading to the ranch, dust spurting high beneath her wheels as she sped up the road. The sun was sinking beneath the mountains in the far distance and the last faint blue of the day was gradually changing to darkness. She floored the accelerator and tore up the drive.

Stopping by the barn, she thrust open the door and hurried out.

Several cowhands were by the fence, watching inside the corral. Holly looked beyond them to see the horse lying down, the two men beside her. She ran to the fence and squeezed through the rails, her bag banging against the lower one.

Sam stood beside Cache, both looking at the little mare. For a stunned moment Holly registered the gun in Cache's hand. She refused to accept what she was seeing, then reality hit her.

'No!' She ran across the soft dirt, slowing as she drew near. The horse was on her side, her front leg twisted and mangled. She was still. At first Holly didn't see the small, dark, bloody hole in the centre of her forehead.

'*No!*' she said again almost as a groan.

Cache turned to stare at her, his face stricken, his eyes dark and anguished.

'Why didn't you wait? I could have saved her.' Holly flung herself down beside the horse, ran her experienced hands over her shoulder, down the leg that was twisted. Warmth met her fingers. Tears streamed down her face. 'Why didn't you wait?' she asked, feeling for a pulse, knowing there would not be one.

'She was always a good horse. I couldn't let her suffer. You couldn't have saved her.' Cache's voice was dull, his eyes almost dead. He stared at the mare, not even looking at Holly.

She stood up and moved to stand before him, ignoring Sam who started to say something, anger flashing through her. She faced Cache, frustrated that he was so much taller than she—frustrated with the entire situation, and so helpless now.

'Dammit, I'm a vet! I should have been allowed to try. I might have saved her. I know what I'm doing, and there are lots of methods now that were not available just a few years ago. You should have given me a chance! Dammit, Cache, you should have given me at least a shot at it! There was no need to kill her. That's not much better than murder!'

Cache swung his gaze from the horse to Holly, but didn't really see her. 'Her leg was too badly broken. It couldn't have been fixed. I think she had internal injuries as well. She was in pain and couldn't get better.'

'You don't know that!' Holly was almost yelling at him. Tears continued to pour down her face as she stared at him accusingly. The ache in her chest was so strong she longed to hit him to vent some of her pain. 'You should have waited; I would have told you if there was nothing to be done. But no, you couldn't wait, the law of the old macho west, put the horse out of its misery. Don't wait for some *woman* who might be able to help.'

His gaze gradually focused on her and he stared at her in growing horror. 'Do you really think that's what this is about? Do you think I wanted to kill her? Sunlight? Because of some macho notion of how to be a cowboy?'

'No, she doesn't think that, boss. Go on now, nothing more to be done here,' Sam said softly, gently nudging Cache, reaching out to pull the gun from his unresisting fingers.

Holly turned to look at the mare, her vision blurred by the tears. She wiped her face and stood still, trying to ease the ache in her heart. And what of her foal? What would the little foal do without its mother? Tears started again. She hated to lose an animal, any animal but most especially horses. But she hated even more that she had not been given the chance to save it.

Cache reached out to grab her shoulders, shaking her lightly. 'Easy, Holly.'

'Easy be damned! How could you?' Wrenching away from him, she moved nearer the horse. Holly took a deep breath. She could hear Cache move across the corral, the soft murmur of the men by the fence as he opened the gate and left.

'Now, Doc, you have no call to yell at Cache. He didn't want to kill Sunlight, But she was in a bad way. You weren't here, we were. She was in pain and you couldn't have fixed her up. I thought maybe you could, but once we saw how bad she was I knew. We're stockmen. We know animals too, Doc.'

'Macho, chauvinistic male,' she muttered, her eyes filling with tears again.

'Now, Doc, not so. That's probably the hardest thing he's ever done. He loved that horse. It has been a favourite of his ever since she came to the ranch. She was Trish's horse.' As if that explained it all.

Holly turned to look at him, tears still shimmering on her lashes. 'Who's Trish?' She had heard that name before.

'Cache's wife.'

She turned to stare down at the dead mare. *Cache's wife*. She'd heard the name several times, but never knew he was married. For a moment she remembered the big bed in the bedroom, too big for a single man. The pain in her chest tightened a little more.

The last of the day's light had gone. As the darkness blanketed the land, Holly could scarcely see the horse any more. She turned and trudged back to the fence, opening the gate and slipping through. Without a word to anyone, she climbed into her jeep and slowly started for home. The ache in her heart was for the horse, and for herself.

It was still and hot when Holly drew up before her house; she didn't go inside. Instead she sat out on the porch, on the long wooden swing that Dr Watson had placed there. Slowly she relaxed, the pain in her chest easing. Tomorrow she'd find out exactly what had happened. She'd have to fill out the records for the county on the death. See what arrangements they wanted for the body. Tomorrow she'd handle all that. For now, she just wanted to sit, and sway with the swing, and not think.

Twice the phone rang. Twice Holly sat swinging, ignoring the summons. The answering machine clicked on and recorded any message. The pager remained silent.

Slowly Holly moved to and fro, endlessly, in the soft, hot night.

She heard the car before she saw the lights. The twin beams slashed through the darkness, the throaty growl filled the silence of the night. She watched as he slowed for her drive and turned in, the arc of the bright light sweeping her yard, briefly illuminating her on the porch before he cut them off. She sat still, watching as he opened the door.

He climbed out and walked up the path to the porch, pausing as he watched her warily then moved to sit gingerly beside her.

'I'm sorry,' she said, before he could speak, her voice tight with tension and unshed tears. It had not been fair of her to attack him, she knew that. She had let her emotions overrule her head.

He sighed softly and pushed back so that the swing started moving.

'I didn't want to, Holly. But she was suffering and there was nothing you could have done about it.'

She nodded, then realised he couldn't see her. 'I just wanted to try.' She was silent for a few moments, then turned to try to see him in the faint starlight. 'Why did you come?'

'You were upset. I tried to reach you by phone, but you didn't answer. I wanted to make sure you were all right.'

'Why?' She'd been offensive, attacking him when he was already down. Rudely accosting him on his own turf. Why had he come to check on her?

'I don't know. Maybe because there was so much sadness, I didn't want you to feel bad tonight.'

'Where's Trish?' Holly bit her lip. She hadn't known she was going to ask that. She wished she had turned on the porch light so that she could see him, see how he took her question.

'Trish died a long time ago, Holly. Sunlight was a present from me to her just before she died. The mare was all I had left of a happy time.'

Holly sat still, assimilating the news. She didn't know whether to be sad Trish was dead, or happy Cache was free. Why did she care? She was only here for the next few months, then she was returning to Kentucky. She couldn't fall for this cocky cowboy. Though he didn't seem very cocky tonight.

He seemed hurt, vulnerable, sad. She could make out his silhouette against the faint light from the stars as he gazed ahead, pushing the swing gently to and fro, lost in thought.

'Cache, do you want to tell me what happened?' she asked softly, afraid to shatter the tenuous peace.

'With Sunlight, or Trish?' he asked, his voice quiet, none of the teasing she was used to hearing. Just a great weariness.

'Either.' Suddenly Holly wanted desperately to learn about Trish. How Cache had loved her, how she'd died, how long ago. Would he ever love anyone again?

'We let Sunlight out in the corral, without Starlight, so she could run and have some sunshine. We had already brought some of the range horses in, in preparation for the drive next week. She was just running; next we saw, she was down. Don't know if she snapped it and then tried to run, or was kicked by one of the other horses. God, I hated to put her down. She was a good horse.'

Holly reached out to touch his arm, her fingers electrified at the touch. His skin was warm, the light covering of hair on his forearm crisp beneath her fingertips. She swallowed hard, aware of him as she had never been before. Time seemed to stand still, her heart sped up and she tried to see him in the darkness.

'I over-reacted when I saw her. I'm sorry I yelled at you,' she said, her fingers tracing patterns on his arm.

'Darlin', if you react like that at every animal's death, you'll burn yourself up in no time.' His voice was gentle.

'I know. But I feel so ineffective. Animals are so helpless; they can't tell you what's wrong.' She'd made a fool of herself, and wanted to explain why.

He reached out and encircled her shoulders with his arm, his fingers trailing lightly along her arm. Holly sighed and leaned against him, relaxing against the soft rhythm of the swing, feeling safe, secure and at peace.

A peace that was short-lived. She could feel his heartbeat as she pressed up against his chest, feel the seductive pressure of his arm across her shoulder, the tingling of her nerve-endings wherever her body touched his, from her arm, to her side, to her thighs. She had trouble breathing, trouble concentrating on anything but the man beside her, and the wonderful fantasies her mind was conjuring.

He'd think her crazy. She tried to slow her breathing, tried to think of the work to be done tomorrow, to think of the cattle drive next week, anything but the male body next to hers, causing her so much havoc. Anything but the shivering delight he brought by his mere touch.

'Holly...'

She turned her face up and he leaned over and kissed her. His lips were warm, but only at first, soon heating up to hot. In only seconds the warmth penetrated her body, his mouth moving against hers, she responding to match pressure for pressure. Loving the feel of his mouth against hers, the movement of his lips tantalising her, tormenting her, delighting her. It was wonderful, but not enough.

She turned slightly to get closer and Cache pulled her into his lap, turning her so that her breasts were pressed against his chest, her legs cradled by his strong thighs. His arms went around her and he pulled her tight against him as his lips moved to open hers and he plunged in to taste the sweet moistness of her mouth.

Holly was on fire, hot, breathless, consumed by the feelings Cache ignited in her. Her fingers traced the strong muscles of his shoulders, the taut column of his neck, the thick hair on the back of his head. She could feel the heat from him at her mouth, relentlessly pursuing, relentlessly giving pleasure beyond anything she'd known.

His chest against hers, his legs beneath hers. All the sensations mingled and imprinted themselves on Holly's mind. She was drifting, floating, lost in a world of sensuous feeling and tactile delight.

His hand moved down her back to her thighs bared by the shorts she wore. She shivered and pressed against him, caught in the storm of his touch. When he slipped beneath the edge of the shorts, she gasped and held her breath.

She thought she would burn up, she was so hot, the night was so hot. Yet she didn't want to change a thing. His hands were magic, his mouth enchanting, his spell catching her fast and binding her to him forever.

The low murmur of the car was lost in the pounding
of blood in her ears. But the sweep of lights across her
lawn shocked Holly to normality. She pulled back and
stared at Cache as he was illuminated briefly by the
passing lights.

CHAPTER SEVEN

CACHE dragged his hands through his hair, warily watching Holly in the darkness, which seemed darker after the car passed.

She moved to sit on the swing, her feet firmly on the porch, her face averted. 'I think it might be best if you go now,' she said softly, watching the tail-lights of the car as it continued away.

'Hell, Holly, I didn't mean for anyone to see us; I wouldn't put your reputation on the line.'

'I know.' Who had driven by? Had he or she seen Cache and her on the porch swing? Or had the driver been concentrating on the road, caught up in his own thoughts?

'Still, it's late.' She was embarrassed. She had enjoyed his kisses and lost herself in his touch. Did he know it?

'Are you OK?'

She nodded, not knowing if he meant because of Sunlight's death, or being caught on the swing. She was surprised; she felt fine. She was sad she couldn't have saved the horse, but knew if Cache and Sam had thought her beyond help she must have been.

And Holly was more alive than ever because of the kisses she and Cache had shared. Lightly she traced her lips with her tongue. There were warm and slightly swollen, and still tasted of Cache McKendrick. Her heart sped up and it was all she could do to keep from throwing herself into his arms again.

'Holly...' What was there to say? He'd come over because he was concerned about her, about her being upset, and instead almost made love to her on the front porch. He couldn't control himself near her. And he had to. He wouldn't go that route again.

'Goodnight, Cache.' Her voice was soft, gentle in the night breeze.

He stood, then turned quickly and stooped for a kiss. His lips barely touched hers before he straightened and strode to his truck, never looking back.

Holly watched as he drove off, watched the road long after his lights had disappeared.

Cache was not at the ranch when Holly drove in the next morning. She finished her work concerning Sunlight, stalling as long as she could in case he'd show up. Finally she had to leave to do the rest of her rounds.

It was hot. The temperature rose into the hundreds, and the air was still. The grass grew drier, bleached almost white, and reflected the heat of the fiery sun. The night had been warm, unusual for this part of the state where usually the evenings cooled off and made sleeping bearable.

Though it had not only been the heat that kept Holly awake last night. Thoughts of Cache had filled her mind, questions about Trish, about him.

She went through her rounds as quickly as she could, longing to return home and change into something cool. She'd get a large drink, find some shade and collapse. It was too hot to be working in the sun. How did the cowboys do it day after day?

When Holly returned home it was late in the afternoon. She was worn out. Dealing with sick animals wasn't the easiest occupation in the world. When those same animals were fractious with the heat, it was even harder.

Emmie met her with a large glass of lemonade, ice tinkling against the sides. Holly gave her a grateful grin and took a big sip.

'Heavenly!' she declared.

'If this heat doesn't break soon, I'll be a prune,' Emmie complained as they entered the house. 'I should have insisted Doc Watson put air-conditioning in. He doesn't care, he's gone all day. I'm surprised his wife didn't insist.'

'Yet we normally don't need it.' Holly finished the lemonade and put down the glass, glancing through the mail stacked on the desk, smiling at Emmie's gentle grumbling.

'It's supposed to stay hot for another couple of days. And nights. That's the worst part.'

Holly nodded absently as she tossed the mail back and moved towards her room.

'I for one am going to change and try to get cool.'

'Take a cool shower, that'll help. I'm off now. Call if you need anything tonight. You still going up with Cache and his crew next week for the branding?'

Holly paused by her door. 'I think so. Hope it cools before that.' Would he want Stan now that he had seen her fall apart? She had tried so hard to prove her worth, only to fail at the first crisis. Shaking her head, she went to take her shower.

Holly went to bed early, to make up for the restless sleep from the previous night. But she couldn't fall asleep. First she was hot. Even with the fan on. Then she couldn't control her thoughts. They centred on a certain roguish cowboy, who constantly invaded her mind. She tried to think about returning to Kentucky, only to have Cache's face dance before her eyes, with his amused eyes, lop-sided grin.

She tried to picture her uncle's reception, his final capitulation to her request to work as a vet for Windmere Farms—only to remember Cache's arms around her as they danced, his teasing voice, the way he always called her 'darlin''. At the thought, her face smiled in remembrance.

'Which means precisely nothing,' she said aloud. Hadn't he called Sally Lambert *sugar*? He was a flirt and a charmer and Holly had best keep her distance.

The phone rang. She reached for the extension by her bed, glancing at the clock as she did so. It was only ten. It felt much later.

'Hello, Doc?'

Cache.

'Yes.' Her heart began pumping stronger. She sat up, conscious of her scanty attire. He couldn't see her, for heaven's sake.

'Are you as hot there as we are out here, darlin'?' His voice was seductive in her ear.

Holly knew she smiled, she couldn't help it. She also felt his tone like a caress throughout her body.

'It is hot,' she replied.

'Come on out here and we'll go riding; we'll cool off some once we get away from the flat land.'

'Cache, it's late. I've already gone to bed.'

'I'll come in there, if you'd rather,' he said quickly.

She grinned, for a moment letting her imagination sparkle with that picture. Reluctantly she denied herself that pleasure.

'No.'

'Maybe another time.'

'I doubt it.'

'Now, darlin', you know we have to start making those exciting memories for you to carry back to Kentucky with you.'

She laughed softly at their nonsense. He'd remembered. She bit her lower lip in indecision.

'All right, I'll come for a quick ride.'

'I can come in and get you.'

'No, I'll drive out in half the time that'd take. I'll be there soon.'

'I'll have the horses waiting.'

When Holly drove into the yard of Cache's ranch, she saw him sitting on the fence near the two horses. They were saddled and ready to go and briefly Holly wondered what they must think of getting all tacked up in the middle of the hot night. For her part she felt wonderful.

In only a few minutes, they were walking up the trail beside the house, heading for the open range.

'It'll be cooler by the river,' Cache said, taking the lead. It was dark; only the light of the stars shed illumination over the land. The horses walked surely, deliberately over the known trail, moving towards the faraway river.

When the trail widened, Holly moved up to ride beside Cache. She knew she was playing with fire, but was drawn to him like a moth to a flame.

'Tell me something about Kentucky, and the allure it has for you, darlin',' Cache said suddenly. 'Your folks live there?'

Holly blinked, startled anew to find his thoughts similar to hers.

'My uncle does, and my cousins. My parents are dead. They died when I was quite small. My uncle Tyson raised me. Just as if I'd been his daughter.'

'He owns a farm?' Obviously Cache remembered their talk on the way to the dance.

'He owns Windmere Farms. He raises thoroughbred horses, races some.'

'And that's where you want to work?'

'Yes, if he'll let me.'

'Why wouldn't he?'

Holly could see that Cache was trying to watch her in the night. His head was turned towards her, but he probably could only see her silhouette, just as that was all she could see of him.

She sighed. 'Uncle Tyson believes a woman should be doing things like shopping, going to teas, or hosting charity balls. Not getting dirty working with horses. When I was small, he'd let me exercise some of them, but once I was in high school he tried to curtail all that activity. I had to be ladylike and not worry myself about horses.'

Some of the anger and bitterness that Holly had felt seeped into her tone. Cache picked it up.

'Yet he let you become a vet.' His voice was gentle.

'No, he didn't. I had to wait until I was twenty-one, then go off to college on my own. I paid my way through school.'

'Quite an accomplishment.'

Holly nodded. It had been an accomplishment, and one of which she was justifiably proud.

'So what does your uncle say now?' Cache asked, reining in his horse as they reached the river.

'Nothing. I haven't spoken to him since I left. Seven years ago.' She looked at the slow-moving water shimmering in the starlight and sighed. 'I'm just hoping he'll let me work there now that I'm qualified and have experience.'

Cache dismounted and dropped his reins, Roman trained to stand. He moved to Holly's side and looked up at her. 'I'll give references, if you like.'

'Even after the scene I made last night?' She tried to see his expression, but his hat blocked even the faint starlight. 'I wasn't even sure you'd want me to go on the cattle drive.' Her voice was lost.

'Yes, I want you.' Cache reached up to her waist and drew her from the horse, sliding her body down the length of his the way he had the other day. Holly's hands were on his shoulders for balance, yet they felt the strength of his muscles, his warmth through the cotton shirt. She was instantly aware of him as her body skimmed his, flaring into awareness, heating up the hot night.

Holly pulled back, stumbled, and recovered her balance. She turned to gaze at the water, trying to keep her racing thoughts under control.

'It's still hot, though a little cooler here,' she said. 'Wish we had a breeze.' Anything to cool her down.

'Want to go swimming?' Cache stood where she'd left him, not moving to follow her as she strolled casually a few steps along the bank.

'I didn't bring a suit,' she said.

He chuckled. 'Neither did I. We can go skinny-dipping.'

'With nothing on?' Her voice was horrified.

Cache chuckled again. 'It isn't as if we could *see* anything; it's dark as hell out here, darlin'.'

Holly shook her head. 'I couldn't.'

Cache moved swiftly until he was before her, looking down at her. 'Are you a prude, or just shy?'

She thought a moment, then raised her face to his. 'I don't think I'm a prude,' she said softly.

'Well, it isn't as if either of us will see anything we haven't seen before,' he said gently, his hands moving to her shoulders, kneading her muscles.

'I might,' she whispered, heat washing through her face.

Cache's hands stilled. The silence went on and on. Holly thought she'd have to say something, move, do something to break the tension that seemed to be rising.

'Holly, have you ever slept with a man?' Cache's voice was low and intense, his hands tightened on her shoulders.

Holly shook her head. 'No,' she said, looking over towards the river.

'But the other day, in the loft...'

'That was quite nice, but I think I got carried away,' she said, embarrassed to have him remind her.

'God! I'll say you got carried away—we both got carried away, and if we hadn't been interrupted by Mrs Eton we would have gotten even more carried away. Dammit, I never suspected you'd still be a virgin.'

Cache moved away from her, his thoughts in turmoil. She had to be in her late twenties, and was still a virgin! His gut tightened and the longing he felt for her the other day surged again.

Holly was embarrassed. She tried to see him in the faint starlight, but could only make out his silhouette. She wished she hadn't told him.

'The water sounds cool spilling over the pebbles,' she said softly, longing to change the subject.

'Keep on your underwear, I'll keep mine on. In this light, it'll be as good as bathing suits,' Cache suggested, turning back towards her.

'Fine.' Holly moved back towards the horses, anxious to put distance between her and Cache, glad for the respite where she could swim and cool off and not have to discuss anything.

The water was a shock; it was cold after the heat of the night. Holly plunged into the pool Cache indicated, where the water was over her head. The current was slow, lazy and she had no trouble swimming in it. Soon her feet touched gravel and sand and she stood, submerged to her neck, as her body cooled and became used to the water.

'It's great!' she called to Cache.

'Knew it would be.' He ducked under the water and soon bobbed up near her. Shaking his head to free it from the water, he sprayed Holly.

'Stop,' she laughed, feeling as carefree as a child.

'Why, darlin', don't you want to get wet? It'll cool you down.' He splashed water over her.

Holly retaliated, skimming her hand along the surface, sending a sheet of water over Cache. In only seconds they were joined in a water battle. She laughed and splashed and tried to avoid the sheets of water he sent her way. A couple of times she got a mouthful of water, which she spat out then splashed back even harder.

Finally she felt she would drown if she couldn't avoid his attacks. Laughing, she held up her hands, half turned away from him to keep the water from her nose.

'Stop, stop, I surrender.' She laughed as the waves of water diminished, and ceased.

'Unconditionally?' Cache demanded, moving slowly through the water towards her, his tone teasing, laughter clearly heard.

'Yes. Gosh, I'll drown if I don't.'

He caught her around the waist and brought her up against his chest, his face on a level with hers. Holly smiled at him, let her feet go and floated in the water, held firm against Cache.

It seemed the most natural thing in the world for Holly to wrap her arms around his neck and kiss him. Her lips touched his tentatively, but when Cache stood still and let her set the pace she increased her pressure, wanting him to respond to her as she always did to him. And he did not disappoint her.

In only seconds, he'd assumed control and moved against her lips in a provocative manner. Holly opened her mouth and Cache's tongue plunged in. Duelling, darting, dancing one against the other, the kiss went on and on. Holly grew warm in the cool water, her mouth craving more of his touch, more of his attention, her lips giving back as good as she got, moving against his, tasting him, touching him.

When Cache eased her away from him, the cool water swirled between them, cooling her instantly. She opened her eyes and stared up at him. Why had he stopped?

'Are you getting cold?' he asked, walking towards the bank.

'Yes.' She was, now that he was no longer pressed against her.

'Get dressed; we'll ride back and have a drink or something before you go.' His voice was colder than before. He kept his hand on her arm to help her up the bank, but his touch was impersonal, his mood distracted.

Holly wondered what had happened to change him so much. One moment kissing her and the next nothing. She raised her chin. She wouldn't ask. If he had second thoughts about her, he needn't explain them to her. She'd get dressed, thank him for the refreshing ride, and return home. Alone!

They said little as they rode back. Holly worried over what had happened to change his feelings towards her. Was it because she was a virgin? Did he only dally with accomplished flirts? A small knot of sadness grew in her chest. She knew she couldn't offer any lasting relationship—she was returning to Kentucky in only a few months. But she enjoyed spending time with him. Enjoyed was too anaemic; she *relished* spending time with him. He was exciting, stimulating, and challenging. He was more than she was used to dealing with, but she'd held her own so far.

When they reached the corral, Cache dismounted easily and reached up for her reins. 'I'll unsaddle them. No point in you getting hot and dusty after your swim.'

She slid off and relinquished the reins. 'Thank you for inviting me.' She smiled shyly, reluctant to end the evening. She didn't know what had gone wrong between them; maybe she should find out.

'Goodnight, Doc.' He turned and led the horses into the barn.

'Cache, wait.' Holly hurried after him. 'Cache, what's the matter? What's wrong?'

'Nothing, Doc, go on home.'

She pulled on his arm, stopping him and turning him a little.

'I want to know what's the matter.'

He stared down at her, his expression one of anger. For a long moment he said nothing, then he leaned over until his face was before hers. 'I'll tell you, then, *darlin'*. I'm a man and you're a woman. A damned beautiful woman, with your soft curves and your shiny brown hair that frames your face like enchantment. I lied: wearing underwear is nothing like a swimsuit. I want you in the most primitive way I know. Having your body against mine in the river was torment beyond what I can stand. You stay away from me, Holly, or I won't be responsible for what happens. I want you more than anything, and if you hang around I'll take you. Any way I can. That's something you can count on.' His face was serious.

Holly stared at him, dumbfounded. She was shocked by his words, by the intensity of his feelings. She could feel the anger and tension in his arm, his muscles taut and tight. She snatched her hand away as if it were burnt. Her heart pounded in her chest, the blood roared in her ears. She had never considered something like this. She liked Cache, was attracted to him as she'd never been to anyone before. But she didn't want to be taken in lust, and he never implied anything else. Slowly she turned and walked towards her car, her head held high, her heart pounding.

'Run away, little girl,' Cache called softly after her. 'But beware if you come back.'

Holly drove home, his words echoing in her head. She'd felt the attraction, should have known he'd want more than a few chaste kisses. And had he not held back she would have given him more. The thought frightened her. She was not someone to go in for casual sex. She wanted love, commitment and the promise of a long life together.

The heat spell broke the next day with a terrific thunderstorm. The rain was fierce but brief and the temperature dropped twenty degrees. Holly worked through the worst of the storm, assisting at a breech birth. The rain reminded her of the water fight she and Cache had indulged in. Immediately she remembered what he'd said afterwards.

For the next few days she avoided any place she thought he might be, avoided anyone who worked with him. Holly didn't want to give him any reason to suspect she was reconsidering, or that she acquiesced in his intentions.

Though she wondered what it would be like to have him kiss her all over, have his hands on her soft skin, bringing her to the edge of ecstasy and beyond, to have him initiate her in the rites of love.

No, no, *no*! She slammed the door on such fantasies. She was leaving heart-whole when she left, and no randy cowboy was going to change that for her.

'Doc, Cache called from the Lone Tree, said something about you going with them on the cattle drive,' Emmie said when Holly returned from her rounds on Tuesday.

'Should I call him back?' Holly asked, anticipation building. She knew the trip was planned for this week. Did he still want her to go?

'Yes. I've packed Doc Watson's sleeping-bag for you. And pulled out the duffel bag he uses when he goes. It's pretty rough in the high country, no modern conveniences.'

'I know. I've done this before.' Holly smiled at the older woman. She was longing to call Cache, to speak to him after so many days. But she hesitated while Emmie was still around. Not that she expected him to discuss anything but business, she told herself.

'I'll call Cache as soon as I write up the files.' She moved to the desk and opened the first patient's file.

Emmie left before Holly was finished, but she forced herself to finish all the write-ups before calling. She was nervous when she dialled, her stomach churning as the phone rang. The let-down was almost physical when Sam answered.

'I was calling Cache about the cattle drive,' Holly said.

'Sure thing, Doc. We leave at sun-up tomorrow. Cache said to tell you to bring a duffel of clothes, dress warmly and he'd take care of the rest. Grub and all.'

'I'll be there by five.' Disappointment warred with excitement as Holly hung up. She hadn't spoken to Cache, but tomorrow she'd see him! Spend several days in his company, working beside him, resting in the evenings with him and his men. A smile lit her features; she was looking forward to it.

It was a few minutes before five when Holly pulled into the yard at the Lone Tree. Yet by the activity going on, one might have thought it closer to midday. Men were everywhere, saddling horses, loading supplies on a serviceable chuck wagon, piling sleeping gear in another wagon, herding horses to swap with when their own mounts grew tired.

Holly no sooner stopped than Cache opened her door and smiled down at her.

'Morning, darlin', you look fresh as a daisy. Ready for this trek?' None of the anger from the other evening showed in his face.

Her heart pounded and her eyes shone her happiness at the day as she nodded. He was dressed in a faded checked shirt, faded blue jeans and old leather chaps. His boots were worn and scuffed but still had years of use ahead.

'Where do you want all my gear?' she asked, still sitting as he was blocking her way.

'Tim!' Cache roared. In only a second one of his hands loped over.

'Take Doc's sleeping-bag and duffel, will you?'

'And the medical supplies?'

'That'll go in the chuck wagon. Anything need refrigeration?'

When Holly shook her head, Cache told Tim to come back for the medical items. He stepped back and Holly climbed down from the jeep.

She wore an old pair of jeans, her boots and a cotton T-shirt beneath a flannel shirt. The morning was cool, now that the heat spell had broken, and while she knew she wouldn't need it later it felt good now.

'You have a hat?' Cache asked.

'Yes.' She reached in for one and put it on. She felt like a true cowboy now.

Cache smiled down at her, teasing lights in his eyes. He reached out and pulled the stampede strap beneath her chin, cinching it snug. 'We'll be doing some hard riding this morning; don't want you to lose it.'

Holly almost jerked away from the tingling awareness his fingers generated. She licked her lips as she stood docilely, hoping he didn't see her heart beating, didn't notice her erratic breathing. Dear God, how would she last a week?

'Ready when you are, boss,' a hand called.

'Right. Mount up.' Cache nodded towards Beau. 'Your horse, madam. Let's go.'

Holly was caught up in the excitement of moving everyone out of the ranch, out to the open range and towards the pastures that supported the cattle. The high range several miles in the distance would be their first stop. After inoculating and branding those cattle that required it there, they'd move to the west, to the long-horns. Holly had only been on one cattle drive before, and knew how hard the work was. But there was still a tremendous satisfaction in the process and she was looking forward to it.

As they spread out across the open range, the men driving the horses moved out ahead as all the horses wanted to run. Holly moved to the side to let them by and continued in their dust, content to ride at a slower pace.

She was not alone. Two or three others ambled along at a slow lope, rather than the hell-for-leather gait of the leaders. Sam rode over to her and told her a little about the set-up to which they were headed.

Before too long, Cache came riding back from the lead. He pulled in beside them, discussing work with Sam, pointing out landmarks to Holly.

They stopped for a quick lunch, then started out again. Again Holly was in the rear, taking her time; her work had not yet started.

As the afternoon waned, she grew tired, and sore from the long unaccustomed hours in the saddle. She'd be glad for the evening's rest. According to Cache, they were to reach their campground around six. That would be their base for the next few days. And she would not need to ride so much as they would herd the cattle, cutting out the ones that needed shots. She only had to get through today.

Holly discarded her flannel shirt, tying it to the back of her saddle. It was hot. She was hot. Lotion on her arms kept her from burning, but she longed for some shade, and a time to just sit and rest.

Cache joined her as they began climbing. The terrain was rising towards the high pasture.

'I'm going to sweep through some of those canyons to the left, Sam's going right. Want to ride along?'

'Sure.' She turned to follow him, her tiredness forgotten. She'd ride anywhere with Cache.

The sage brush grew to the height of Holly's knees even on Beau. As they wound their way through some of the thick sage, branches slapped against her legs, pulled as if trying to dislodge her. She knew why Cache wore the chaps. Maybe she'd get some before doing anything like this again. If she ever did anything like this again. For a moment she thought of Kentucky. There was nothing like this in Kentucky.

Cache spotted a couple of steers and headed in their direction, turning them towards the base camp, moving them in their slow, ambling way. Once they were started, he continued on, eyes constantly searching the land for more.

'What if they turn around?' Holly asked as she pushed Beau to catch up.

'They'll probably drift, but they'll be headed generally in the right direction. We'll check out this canyon, then double back and keep them on track. You holding up OK?'

'I'm a little tired, but doing OK.'

He smiled and nodded. 'You'll do.' With a nudge, Roman started forward. They searched one canyon, then moved to another. Several times Holly spotted the red cattle, and moved to push them towards the camp. Several were yearlings.

The afternoon was waning. Cache seemed tireless and Holly pushed to keep up with him.

She swung wide, looking for more cattle. In one of the gullies they criss-crossed, she spotted three. Urging Beau down, they started across the dry stream bed, heading for the cattle. Loping along, suddenly Beau stumbled, fell. Caught off guard, Holly slipped from the saddle, over his head, landing hard on the baked ground.

CHAPTER EIGHT

HOLLY held on to consciousness as the blackness around the edges faded back to daylight. She could see Beau standing a few feet away, but the banks of the gully rose above her to hide any long-distance view. Where was Cache? She sat perfectly still for a moment, assessing any damage. Except for a slight headache, she seemed fine. Gingerly she tried sitting up.

The pounding of Roman's hoofs sounded on the dry ground and Holly looked over her shoulder to see Cache riding hard. He was out of his saddle in seconds, leaning over her.

'God, Holly, are you all right?' His face mirrored his concern, his fear.

'Yes, I think so. Boy, what a spill. Is Beau OK?'

'I don't know; what happened?' He reached down to draw her up, watching to make sure she could stand before turning to glance at Beau.

'Thought you said you could ride.' His face mocked her, his eyes twinkled in amusement, relief evident in his expression as she walked slowly over to the horse standing patiently.

'Ohhh!' She was instantly furious and turned on him, her hands on hips. 'Of course I can ride; I wasn't expecting him to stumble. Neither was Beau. Thanks for your concern.'

Cache's face grew serious. 'I was concerned, but you're fine. Let's see how he is.'

131

'I'm sorry, Cache, I didn't mean to fall.' Her tone eased a little. She brushed back a few tendrils of hair that drifted around her face, discovering the small lump where she'd hit the ground.

'I'm just surprised you did, stumble or not.' He reached the horse and rested his hand on his rump, checking him over. Holly passed him, running her hands over Beau's forelegs, feeling his forefeet. She winced at the swelling she felt, studying the left leg.

'Does it hurt, old fellow?' she said softly, her hands gentle on the horse. Standing, she turned to Cache. 'I think it's just a bad sprain; he must have hit a chuckhole. I don't think it's broken, but he shouldn't walk any more today than he has to. And probably not be ridden for a few days. How far are we from camp?'

He looked around and back to Holly, his face serious. 'A couple of hours or more. If someone doesn't come looking for us, I don't know how far Roman can carry us both. He's had a hard day, and it's uphill to the camp.' He didn't have to say it was even further back to the ranch. Holly knew how much distance they'd covered that day.

'I don't think Beau should walk a long way on that leg. You ride on, get help and come back for me.' She wasn't worried about being alone for a few hours.

'It would be dark before I could get back. I might miss you and you'd be out all night alone. It'll get cold tonight. I'm not leaving you.'

As if to prove his words, a slight breeze blew across Holly's face, the air cool. She glanced around. There was very little shelter on the open range. They were some distance from the slope of the hill they needed to cross, though there were some large boulders there. Around

them was only the dried grass and silvery sage of the
high desert. Nothing to keep the breeze from blowing
or to hold warmth.

'Is that all you have to keep warm?' Cache looked at
her T-shirt.

'I have a flannel shirt tied on to the saddle. I'll be all
right.'

'Like hell you will. We're at a much higher elevation
than town. And that heat spell broke. It'll get cold up
here tonight. Let's find a place to hole up.' He reached
for Beau's bridle and continued as he walked back towards his horse.

'We can ride double for a short distance. We'll ride
towards the hills and look for a sheltered place against
the night wind. Beau can go that far, can't he?'

She nodded, watching as he grabbed Roman's reins
and then easily swung into his saddle. When he was set,
he motioned for Holly to come closer, then reached down
his hands and clasped beneath her arms. Holly was conscious of his warmth against her sides, his palms
skimming the edge of her breasts. She took a breath;
now was not the time to be thinking of such a thing. She
had to get on the horse.

'On three, spring up,' he said, his voice low and calm.

She nodded, her hands on his arms, her eyes on his.
All she could think of was his hands against her body,
the warmth emanating from them. Their proximity to
her breasts, which were beginning to ache with longing.

'. . . three.'

Springing up, Holly was pulled up to sit sideways
before Cache. He slid back as far as he could go and
she swung her leg over the horse and sank into the valley
between the saddle horn and Cache's strong thighs. His

right arm came round beneath her breasts and took up the reins.

Holly held herself as stiffly as possible, not wanting to give in to the urge to lean against him, to feel the strong muscles of his chest support her. The muscular warmth of his legs and arm were almost more than she could tolerate. Her body longed for his; she wanted to feel his mouth against hers again, feel his hands on her skin, see what pleasure he could offer her. She tried to hold herself away from him.

'Relax.' He shook her gently. 'You're too stiff; move with Roman.' Cache pulled her back against him as the horses began walking, picking their way through the sage, over the rocks heading towards the ridge, slowly so that Beau could keep up.

Holly tried to comply, tried to relax and move with the horse, but she could only think of the man holding her. His chest muscles moved against her back as he directed the horse, kept Beau's reins firmly in hand, the heat of his arm burning a band beneath her breasts, sending tingling waves of awareness throughout her body. Her bottom rested against his thighs and she could feel those muscles move as he guided Roman.

Shifting slightly, trying to put distance between them, she gradually became aware of the change in Cache. She froze.

'Dammit, darlin', you've got to sit still. I get hard just thinking about you, and with your soft little bottom moving around like that I'm more than thinking about you.'

'Sorry.' Her voice came out thready, hesitant. Her body shot through with heat and she could only think of Cache, what it would be like to have him touch her

all over, give in to the desire that sprang up between
them whenever they were close to one another.

The excitement of the cattle round-up was forgotten.
Even Windmere Farms was forgotten as Holly could only
concentrate on the man she rode with. For a few moments she let her mind take off in a flight of fantasy,
only to jerk herself up short when she realised where her
thoughts were leading. Dangerous thoughts. She had to
remember where she was headed.

She shifted a little, and heard Cache groan behind her.

'God, Holly, you're driving me crazy!'

'Sorry,' she said again, swallowing hard, wondering
what he thought he was doing to her! 'I didn't mean to,'
she added softly.

'Here we are, you plastered as close to me as you can
get with clothes on, your legs against mine, your soft
bottom doing crazy things to me, and your breasts heavy
against my arm. I'd like to turn my hand over and
capture one, hold it in my hand, see how it fits; reach
under that cotton shirt of yours and feel the satin touch
of your skin, feel it against my hand the way I did once
before.'

Holly was drowning in sensations. As he said each
word, she pictured him touching her, her body against
his, his hands on her, caressing her, bringing her the delight she'd caught a glimpse of in the barn. Her heart
was pounding and heat flooded her being. She couldn't
talk, only move back against him a bit, as if encouraging him in his pursuit.

Cache's left hand nuzzled the edge of her shirt, slipping
beneath it to stroke slowly the soft skin covering her
ribs. Holly caught her breath. The feeling was exquisite.
She wanted more. Opening her mouth for better venti-

lation, she sighed softly and relaxed completely against him.

When his hand moved up, she held her breath again, waiting for the moment he'd touch her breast, slip beneath her bra and rub his rough fingers against her soft skin.

Roman stumbled. Cache gripped the horse with his legs, and pulled his hand from beneath her shirt.

'We've gone far enough. He's tired and I don't want him to get injured.'

'Right.' She could scarcely speak. The sun was sinking fast against the western horizon and the shadows were already long. Cache headed towards a tall boulder, pulled in the horses and dismounted.

Reaching up, he lifted Holly down from the saddle, his eyes teasing, his body taut and tantalising. The friction was alluring and Holly smiled sassily up at him, determined he'd never know how much he affected her.

'That was deliberate,' she said, stepping back.

'Yes, and fun, too.'

She agreed but didn't say a word.

Cache turned to his horse and Holly moved to unsaddle Beau. She checked his leg again, noting the swelling and the scrape on his leg. There was nothing further she could do without her instruments, and she wished she'd brought her bag with her.

She carried the saddle towards the large boulder. It was still warm from the afternoon sun and felt good against her back as she sat and leaned against it.

'Now what?' she asked when he'd taken the saddle off Roman and hobbled him near by.

'Now we wait for morning.'

Cache drew together dead branches of sage and piled the wood near them, using some to build a small fire.

'When it's going good, it'll give us some heat, reflected from that rock. Then we can lie down and sleep in a warm spot.'

'How did you learn that?'

'Read about it in a Western once.'

'And do you fancy Westerns?'

Cache looked up, his eyes looking deep into hers and his head slowly shook. 'What I fancy, darlin', is you.' He reached his hand out and threaded his fingers through her hair, pulling her closer so that his mouth could cover hers.

Holly never thought to protest. She longed to feel his lips, to experience again the delight she felt in his arms— to store up exciting memories to last her whole life through, once she returned to Kentucky.

Eagerly she met his embrace, her arms coming up to encircle his neck and shoulders, to trace the movement of his muscles as he brought her closer to him, pressing her soft breasts against the iron-hard muscles of his chest. Her mouth opened to receive the assault of his, sighing in delight as his tongue invaded the softness of her mouth, the sweetness within.

Cache pulled back, his eyes glittering down at hers, yet he slowly eased her away from him. Holly was puzzled as he sat back.

'I'm not going to start something I can't finish. And I have the distinct feeling you would want more than one night in California's high desert.'

'You're right,' she said softly, moving around to face the small fire, disappointed.

'But you're going back to Kentucky to find that special unending relationship,' he said, watching her.

'I'm going back to be a vet at Windmere Farms. If I find a special unending relationship, so much the better.' She tilted her chin at him.

'What if it's all changed?' he asked gently.

'I don't know. I'm hoping my uncle will let me work there. I don't know what I'd do if he still says no. I've been planning this for seven years.' Holly smiled a little. 'It's been my driving goal for so long, I just don't know what I'd do if I couldn't go back and work as a vet for Windmere Farms.'

'You'd find another goal.'

'Hmm, maybe.' She fell silent, not wanting to think along those lines. For a moment she was scared. What if things hadn't changed? What if her uncle still thought she should go to dinners and dances and not mess about the stables? What if he still refused to let her work as a vet?

Holly was surprised to find that the thought didn't upset her as much as she thought it should. Cache was right, she'd find another goal. Had she grown up somewhere along the way?

She'd still be a vet, and a good one. She'd be able to work with horses or cattle, or whatever took her fancy.

She slanted a look at Cache beneath her lashes. He fancied her. She knew it. But he never said anything about liking, or loving. Would it make a difference to her if he loved her? Her heart sped up and her stomach suddenly was full of butterflies. Ruthlessly she damped down the thought. She was not going to fall for some cowboy, no matter how sexy. She was going to return to Kentucky!

'What about you, Cache? If Trish died so long ago, why haven't you married again?'

He flicked her a glance. 'Don't plan to marry again. Didn't work the first time.'

'You can't help that Trish died,' she said, surprised at his answer.

He sighed and looked back at the fire. He was silent so long she thought he wasn't going to speak again. But he did.

'You remind me a little of Trish. She was a city girl, more at home at dances and nightclubs and the concert halls than on a ranch. She pined for the city. We were happy at first, but after a few months she was discontented and bored. We didn't have much money then, so I couldn't afford to give her the trips she wanted.'

'Of course not, you were just starting out.' Holly remembered how long he'd owned the ranch—only a decade. He'd done so much it was hard to remember he'd done it in that relatively short time.

'Sounds practical, but she didn't want to be practical. She wanted bright lights and fun and excitement. It was hard trying to build up a ranch. Even today I don't have a lot of cash. And I'm doing much better than we ever did. But I still don't have money for travelling all around.'

'So she was unhappy,' Holly said softly, her heart aching for him. He must have loved her so much and she could hear the hurt in his voice when talking about her.

'Yeah. Everyone thought we were the perfect couple, young, starting out, happy. But it was a façade. We had some real yelling matches.'

He looked over at Holly. 'I've not told too many people this, but she was killed when she was leaving me. And I wasn't sad to see her go.'

She widened her eyes in shock. She'd never expected that!

Cache saw her startled look and shrugged, turning back to the fire, his face set in bitter lines. 'So, knowing I can't make a woman happy, I'll not try again. I've got a younger brother. He or his kids can inherit the ranch when I'm gone. I'm not going through all that again,' he said.

Holly didn't know what to say. She'd thought he had worshipped Trish so much that he couldn't look at another woman, but the reality was quite different. Cache wasn't avoiding other women because he couldn't forget Trish, he was avoiding them to avoid a problem like he'd found with Trish.

'But Cache, not all women are like Trish. You could find someone else, have a big family and a lot of happiness. There are lots of women who would love to live on a ranch.'

'You for one?' he challenged her.

For a moment Holly wondered if she wanted to stay. Was the dream of the last seven years worth it? If he asked her to stay, would she consider it? Before she could seriously answer the question, he spoke again.

'Forget it, darlin'; are you warm enough?' he firmly changed the subject.

'Yes, thank you.' She shivered slightly in the cool night air, drawing her flannel shirt on, buttoning it up to the collar. The sky was dark, scattered light from the stars reflected dimly down on the open range and the night air cooled quickly. Holly rubbed her arms, getting a little warmth from her hands. It was cooler now than earlier, and yet still early. How much colder would it get before dawn?

'Sorry, no food.'

'I don't have any either,' she said, watching the greedy flames attack the dry wood. Soon the warmth reached her. Holly looked across the fire at Cache, wondering about him. How badly had he been hurt by Trish? Was he serious in never wanting another try at love, just because one hadn't worked?

If she loved someone, she'd do anything she could to be with them, make them happy. But if it didn't work out, would she turn her back on other chances? She stared into the flames, trying to find the answer.

'You'll go blind, staring into the light,' Cache said, watching the flickering light on her face. She was lovely!

Holly looked up and stuck out her tongue. 'You sound like a mother. I'm fine. People gaze into fires all the time. They're mesmerising. Besides, it's the only light; where else should I look?' I could look at you, she thought, all night.

'Tell me about your uncle, and your cousins,' Cache said.

'If you tell me about your folks, and your brother who stands to inherit a vast ranch.'

Cache chuckled at that. 'Hardly vast. But sure, I'll let you in on all the family secrets.'

For the next few hours they discussed their families, finding similarities and differences. Cache's family had been ranchers for generations. What was surprising was that he'd branched out on his own. His father's spread was still a going concern and he could have worked there.

'But I wouldn't have been top dog. So I got my own spread.'

'I'm sure you always wanted to be top dog. You could have been when you inherited your dad's ranch.'

'Hell, Holly, if he lives to be ninety, I'd be in my late sixties. Too long to wait.'

Holly explained about her uncle and his old-fashioned ideas of her being a southern belle, never dirtying her hands with stable work. Explained some of her frustration at not being able to do what she wanted, not being taken seriously, as her cousins were.

'But you'll change all that, won't you?' Cache said softly, as Holly gave a huge yawn.

She nodded, her gaze drifting back to the fire. She was warm, and content. She didn't need food or a house, just warmth and this man near her.

Cache rose and picked up his saddle and dropped it between the fire and the boulder. Taking the saddle blanket in hand, he motioned to Holly. 'Lie down here. You can use the saddle as a pillow. With the fire on one side and the boulder on the other it'll be as warm as we'll get.'

'I don't want to be covered with that blanket; it smells of horse.' She wrinkled her nose.

'Better than freezing to death. Besides, you've smelled worse.' His lop-sided grin tugged at her heart. Cache sat down and patted the ground beside him. 'Come on.'

Watching him warily, she moved to sit beside him. 'Now what?'

'Lie down.' Cache lay back, his head on the saddle, and gathered her against him, dropping the heavy horse blanket over them, his arm coming around her.

Holly felt warmer instantly. 'Is this what being a cowboy is like?' she murmured, growing sleepy now that she was warm. Trying to ignore the hunger that gnawed at her stomach, she wished she had at least brought a candy bar. This wasn't turning out the way she'd thought it would, but maybe it was even better. She was enjoying herself, she discovered in surprise.

Cache chuckled. 'Not usually. It's rare I sleep with anyone on the range.'

She smiled at the thought and moved closer. In only a moment she closed her eyes, listening to the sounds of the night—the fire crackling merrily near by, the breeze rustling through the sage, soft scampering noises as the night animals went about their business. Soon she slept.

Cache felt her relax when she fell asleep and smiled into the night. He pulled her closer, fitting her body against his from shoulder to thigh. She smelled fresh and clean even after a day of riding. If he couldn't have her the way he wanted, this would have to do. It was late before he slept.

When Holly awoke the next morning, Cache was up and moving around. She must have stirred slightly, though, because he looked over at her almost immediately.

'How are you feeling?' he asked.

The sun was already up, and the early morning chill dissipated. She saw Roman bridled and standing, awaiting the saddle. Beau was near by, cropping on some weeds. Looking again at Cache, she noticed the faint beard, golden hair glinting in the sun, and smiled.

'I'm hungry, thirsty and wish I could have a shower. Other than that I'm having fun on your camp-out.'

He smiled back. 'You're a good sport, Holly.'

She sat up, pushing off the horse blanket with a grimace. It had kept her warm in the night, but she didn't like smelling like a horse.

'Hey, I'm your vet. This goes with the territory. You'd expect the same from Dr Watson, wouldn't you?' She stood up and stretched out some of the kinks. Her back was stiff from sleeping on the hard ground. She was a little surprised she'd slept as well as she had.

'I probably would not have shared my saddle and blanket with that doctor,' Cache said. 'Let's get going. We'll see how far this old fella can take us today.' He quickly saddled Roman while Holly tacked up Beau, leaving the girth loose; he'd carry no riders this morning.

Cache scattered the fire, making sure there were no embers. 'Ready?'

'Sure.'

'You get up and then I'll get on behind you.'

'OK. Sounds like fun.'

'Behave yourself today,' he ordered.

'I always do.' With that Holly reached up and clasped her hands behind his head, bringing him down so that she could brush a kiss across his lips.

With a soft groan, Cache caught her mouth with his and kissed her long and hard. She was smiling when he drew back.

With a scowl, he lifted her up and put her in the saddle. Without another word, he mounted behind her, gathered Beau's reins, and set off.

Holly knew better than to press her luck, so she kept silent, but smiled in pure pleasure when his arm came around her and held her back against him.

They had been travelling for half an hour or so when they spotted another rider coming down the hill in the distance. It was Sam, and he was leading another horse.

'Rescued,' Holly murmured. 'I hope he brought food.'

Cache urged Roman towards Sam and in only moments they met.

Sam had known something was wrong when Cache had not joined the camp before dark. He'd set out at first light to find them, bringing another horse, just in case.

'Knew you'd be OK with Cache out here,' he said as he finished his explanation. Holly wondered what OK meant. She thought about their time around the fire, the stories shared, the contentment she'd felt. Yes, she was OK with Cache.

Without a word, Cache dismounted, assisted her down and, taking Beau's saddle, soon had Holly mounted on the new horse.

Sam tossed them each an apple, and they started towards the camp. Holly kept quiet as the men talked about the night, about the work that was started, and how many more cattle might be in the canyons and breaks around.

Cache ignored her when they reached camp, letting her get off the horse herself. None of the body-to-body contact of the previous day. It was as if she were Dr Watson, she mused as he turned away and quickly moved to see what the men were doing.

She hurried over to the chuck wagon, grateful for the coffee the cook offered her. So much for Cache's attention. But he was the boss, had a lot to do and think about and she would do well to remember that.

The next few days were busy. Holly helped where she could, inoculating the cattle, checking them for para-

sites or disease, assisting in some of the branding and
ear-notching. Once in a while she'd noticed Cache staring
at her, but usually something would come up to draw
her attention, and when she'd look again he'd be busy
elsewhere.

Tired at the end of each day, Holly did her best to
blend into the evening routines. She did not want anyone to complain because a woman was along. She was
the vet, plain and simple.

On the afternoon of the fourth day they were pre-
paring to move to another area of the range, having finished with the cattle in that sector. She brushed out her
hair after lunch, and rebraided it down her back. A quick
wash and she was as fresh as she was going to get until
she got home. She loaded her things in the wagon and
went to get her horse. Beau had improved with rest, but
she still didn't want to put him to strenuous use. She
took the other horse, Tomahawk.

Everyone was breaking camp, saddling his horse and
packing up. She readied her mount, then moved out of
the commotion, to the edge of the camp. They were on
a high plateau and she could look over the valley, see
Mount Shasta in the distance, rising out of the plains in
the afternoon light.

'You look as if you just stepped from a bandbox,'
Cache's voice sounded in her ear.

Holly spun around and smiled up at him, pleased he
had taken a moment to stop and talk with her—she felt
she'd not seen him for days. He came around the horse
and stood near her, his back to the view, trapping her
between her horse and his own broad chest. She liked
her new view better.

He wore a checked shirt, unbuttoned and hanging from his shoulders, admitting a tantalising glimpse of his broad chest, deeply tanned from work in the sun. His beard was several days old, and looked like fine gold glinting in the sun. Her fingers tingled with wanting to touch it, to see if it was as soft as it looked. His eyes were a deep blue, their mocking gaze evident as he looked down at her.

'Kind of you to say so. I thought you'd forgotten I was here.' Instantly she coloured, angry that she'd given herself away. He was busy working, for heaven's sake, not out here to entertain her.

'Oh, no, darlin', I haven't forgotten for a moment you were here. Not during the day, nor during any of the long nights.'

'It's been busy.' She floundered for something to say, keeping her eyes resolutely on his, avoiding the temptation of reaching out to touch him, though her fingers ached with just such a desire.

'But not too busy to watch you. And see you watching me.' His voice was low, his lop-sided smile melted Holly's heart. She took a shaky breath, not wanting to change a thing.

Cache reached around her and rested his hand on her saddle, enclosing her even closer in a small world of their own. The horse shifted his weight and stood still; Cache moved closer, his head tipped down towards her so that his hat sheltered her from the sun. His eyes lost their teasing look. Instead, Holly recognised hunger in their depths.

She reached out her hand to keep him away, her fingers almost scalded by the feel of his skin as her hand made contact. Without thought, her fingers traced the muscles of his chest, brushed lightly over one brown nipple.

Cache drew in a sharp breath, his hands clenching, his gaze narrowing as he stared down into Holly's dreamy eyes.

'Do you know what you're doing?' he asked in a harsh voice.

She licked her lips and shook her head slightly, only knowing she didn't want to stop.

'What I'd like to do is take you off into the hills somewhere, away from all these guys, for a few hours. Just you and me. I'd strip your clothes from your delicate little body and kiss every inch of your skin. Then taste you all over, then make slow, hot love to you, until we couldn't do it any more.'

Holly felt a delicious weakness invade her limbs; her knees grew weak and her body warmed at his words. She stared, mesmerised, into his eyes, the blue deep and dark and passionate, the hunger evident. Her mind took flight at the images he evoked. Her breasts and stomach began to tingle in anticipation. For a long moment she forgot about Kentucky, forgot about his reluctance to get involved with anyone. It would be glorious making love with Cache; why not?

'When are you going to do us both a favour and sleep with me before you take yourself off to Kentucky? The memories we make will keep you warm when you get home, and dammit, Holly, I want you and I know you want me. Can you deny it?'

No, she couldn't, not without lying both to him and herself. Her fingers continued to caress the warm skin of his chest even as her mind leaped ahead to the picture he'd painted. She did want him, she didn't understand it; it was not destined to be a long-term relationship on either part. But she had never wanted to make love with a man the way she wanted Cache McKendrick. They would hurt no one if they slipped away. She had no one, nor did he.

CHAPTER NINE

WHEN Holly didn't respond, Cache caught her chin in
his left hand and tilted her face gently, his hand slipping
down to caress her throat, his thumb drawing feather-
light strokes along her jaw. Slowly he lowered his head,
his mouth hovering scant inches above hers, his breath
mingling softly with hers. Holly could scarcely breathe.

'Tell me if you don't want me,' he repeated again,
then covered her lips with his before she could answer.

Holly opened her mouth and eagerly responded to his
kiss as she hadn't to his question. Her tongue duelled
and danced with his. She strained to get closer, moving
to encircle him around his waist, her hands tracing patterns on his bare back, beneath the loose shirt. Learning
him, sculpting him, wanting to get even closer. She was
hot, and it had nothing to do with the sun beating down
on them—this heat came from within, came from the
flames Cache was igniting within her.

His hand could feel her pulse in her throat, and he
kept his fingers lightly against that slender column, caressing, gauging, tormenting. Though his touch was light,
it was as if it paralysed her; she couldn't breathe, couldn't
think, could only feel his touch.

'Hey, boss, you going to hang around here all day?'

Cache raised his head, looked over Holly, over her
horse to Sam. His expression darkened, then he took a
deep breath. 'No, I'm not. Everyone ready?'

Sam nodded and glanced around. Most of the other
men were already moving out, the chuck wagon had

lumbered past and the few hanging around were watching
Cache, knowing grins wide on their faces.

'Damn,' he said softly.

'Damn is right. I have enough trouble having people
think I'm competent as a vet without everyone in Waxco
thinking I let the cowboys maul me,' Holly said, ducking
from under his arm and yanking the horse's reins. She
was over-reacting, she knew, but she was embarrassed
to be caught out, with everyone watching. She needed
to guard against that kind of thing, but when around
Cache she forgot everything.

Cache jerked back to avoid being hit by the horse's
head, then glared after her, his temper flaring.

'It takes two, darlin'. I didn't see you beating me away.
Besides, everyone doesn't think you let anyone maul you.
Maybe they know you're mine.' He stood straight, his
legs spread apart, his fists on his hips.

'Don't be a dog in the manger, Cache,' Holly said,
mounting her horse and leaning down so that he could
hear her. 'You don't want me except for a toss in the
hay. You don't want any long-term commitment, remember? The whole town knows that. Stay away from
me. I'm here to work.'

She turned and kicked the horse, taking her frustration out on that poor animal. Tomahawk started off
at a swift trot and when Holly gave the sign broke into
a lope. It wasn't his fault, she was mad at Cache. The
man was infuriating! But he'd made it perfectly clear he
didn't want her and that was fine with her. Wasn't it?

Yes! She was going back to Kentucky in a few months.
She didn't have time for some dumb cowboy who was
too afraid of repeating the past to give the future a
chance, who judged all women by one. One moreover
who was dead and gone.

She ignored the small voice that asked what she'd been thinking of a few moments before, when he'd tried to talk her into lovemaking. How appealing it had sounded, how enticing. She was here to work and work she would. When the cattle drive was over, she'd be heart-whole and fancy-free.

But even as she rode out into the morning, a small voice inside called her a liar.

Working with the longhorns was different from with the Herefords. The descendants of early Texas cattle were bad-tempered and difficult. Everyone had to exercise much more care around them than the other cattle. Holly watched carefully, did her job and stayed away from the main body of the herd, and from Cache.

Every time she saw him coming, she'd latch on to Tim or Larry or Sam and start a discussion. She'd keep her attention on whatever topic they discussed, though every nerve-ending was attuned to Cache. She knew he was watching her, and a small glow of satisfaction engulfed her at the thought. He wasn't as indifferent to her as he claimed. But she kept her distance. He was too dangerous, too tempting.

Cache let her get away with it, but his eyes followed her, knowing and patient. He would stand and watch her and whomever she was talking to. Holly felt his eyes on her and would toss her head, as if she didn't have a care in the world, but he knew she knew, and it amused him—when it didn't drive him crazy.

Every time she was tempted to give in and go to him, her pride would rear up. He'd been honest with her— he didn't want anything more than a toss in the hay. And she knew better than to let herself be talked into that. At least she thought she did. But at night in her sleeping-bag, with the stars overhead and the fire burning merrily near by, she'd remember his soft voice, the image his words suggested when he proposed they slip away, and her body would yearn for him, and her soul.

Four days later the drive ended and Holly and the men headed for the ranch house and home. The last of the calves had been branded, those needing inoculations had received them. It was time to wind down and return to day-to-day routine.

The pace back was slow, talk desultory. Even the remuda horses walked along, no longer running with fresh energy. The excitement of change from a week ago had dampened now with all the hard work that had been required. The next drive would start off full of energy, too, she knew.

Holly was bone-weary. She had pushed and pulled and inoculated and notched and castrated more steers than she could count. She had done her fair share and was satisfied with the job done, knowing Dr Watson could not have done better. While horses were her first love, she liked working with cattle, and had enjoyed herself tremendously, learned some things, and felt more confident in her abilities. She was glad she'd chosen her field and knew she would continue to do well in the profession.

But for now she was ready to go home, to a hot bath, a quiet house and a soft bed. Get away from dirt and horses and hard sleeping-bags. Away from the turmoil of cattle, cowboys and Cache.

'So you survived.' Sam rode up beside her and reined in his horse to match her gait.

'Appears I have.' She smiled at him. 'And had a grand time to boot.'

He chuckled, shook his head. 'Hardest work there is, and you had a grand time. Don't figure. But you did us proud, Doc. I was glad you came along.'

'Thanks.' She shifted a little in the saddle, trying to ease aching muscles, thinking of the long, hot bath she planned to have once she was home. Her muscles were sore, her hair gritty with dirt and dust, and she was tired! It was going to be the best appreciated bath in her life—if she could just stay awake long enough to enjoy it!

'You and the boss getting on OK?' Sam asked after a moment.

Her head turned to him. 'Why do you ask?'

'Hell, he's as grouchy as an angry grizzly and you avoid him like he was carrying the plague.' He shrugged, 'Just wondering, that's all.' Sam threw her a look under his brim.

'Except for the fact your boss doesn't want to get involved with any woman, unless it's just to take her to bed, everything is just fine,' she snapped out, angry that even though she wasn't looking for a long-term relationship either Cache made no bones about not wanting one from her.

'He had a hard time with Trish. He's a little gun-shy.'

'Well, it's time he remembered I'm not Trish.'

Sam looked at her for a long moment, then nodded his head. 'I guess you're right. Trish would never have come on a drive like this, much less stuck it out. She'd never have offered to help in any way. You two ain't alike at all.'

'Too bad Cache can't keep that in mind.' That was his problem, he couldn't forget Trish, and compared all women to her. Well, he was wrong. Not that it mattered, but he should remember that.

'Give him some time, Doc, he'll come around,' Sam said.

'He can have all the time he wants, but I'm leaving for Kentucky in a few months. Once Dr Watson returns.' She said it loud and clear, almost defiantly. Everyone needed to remember she was only here temporarily. Especially herself.

Holly managed to avoid Cache at the ranch, in all the confusion and commotion. Keeping a wary eye on him as he moved among his men, gave directions, orders, she quickly unsaddled her horse and brushed him down. Sam took care of the feed, and Holly went to check Beau one last time. Satisfied that he was healing as he should be, she slipped out to get into her jeep.

Eyeing it as she approached, she gave a small smile. It was dirty, dusty and looked as if it were five years old. It fitted right in with the other vehicles around the barnyard and gave her a feeling of belonging. Maybe she should give it a wash, but not today. She just wanted to get home. She was gone before she saw Cache again.

The mail was stacked up on the desk, the house hot and stale when she entered. There was a note from Emmie about fresh food in the refrigerator. She noted it all in passing as she headed for the bathroom.

Fresh and clean after a long, hot soak, Holly fixed a light supper and sat down to read her mail. The letter on top was from Dr Watson. Emmie must have recognised his handwriting. Wondering what he would be writing about, she slit open the envelope and withdrew the page. Her eyes widened in surprise at the words written there.

Dr Watson was offering to sell her part of his practice!

He wanted to make more frequent visits to his children and grandchildren and wondered if she was interested in buying into partnership with him for the time being, with an option to buy the entire practice at a later date. He'd heard some good things about her and was interested in a deal.

Holly re-read the letter, unbelieving. It was a generous offer, especially when she had never met the other vet personally, only corresponded by mail. Who had he been talking to? Emmie? Cache?

It was a grand opportunity. Only... she paused and stared out of the window... she was returning to Kentucky. If she didn't have that, she might consider staying in Waxco and accept Dr Watson's offer. For a moment she let herself indulge in daydreams, of her staying, Cache finding out and...

Enough of that. He'd made it plenty clear that he wanted her but not forever. He was counting on her leaving. If she stayed, she'd bet he'd change his tune fast enough. And she would never be like Sally Lambert, chasing after some man who didn't want her.

She slowly laid the letter aside and read the rest of her mail. But the idea stayed in the back of her mind.

The next morning she kept office hours. She was busy with dogs and cats and pet lambs. She'd been gone for over a week and as these patients weren't critically ill or injured their owners had decided to wait for her to return, rather than visit Stan Connors over in Overilla. She recognised a few of the owners and chatted briefly with them. For a moment she considered what her life would be like if she stayed. It was nice to know people, feel as if she belonged. As one of the town's vets, she would have a place of respect. A sense of belonging. And she'd already made a start on it.

But she used to belong at Windmere Farms. Once back there, she'd fit right in again.

It was after lunch when Holly heard the familiar truck in the driveway. She was glad she still wore the lab coat—it gave her a feeling of authority. And she needed every bit of it against the overwhelming magnetism of Cache McKendrick. She walked to the door and waited for him as he walked up the path.

'Hello.' She pushed open the screen and Cache stepped into the front room, immediately filling it with his presence. Holly felt the strong pull of attraction despite her feelings of the last few days of the drive.

'How are you doing? No lasting effects from the drive?' He stopped close enough to her that Holly had to tilt her head back to see him, her lips tingling at the thought that he might kiss her.

'No, I'm fine.' She blinked and stepped back, dropping her eyes lest he see the desire displayed there. Why was he here?

'I think Emmie would have billed you,' she offered.

'I wanted to see you.' He swept his hat off, running his fingers through his dark blond hair. It was a little long; soon he'd need to get it cut. His cheeks were smooth—gone was the beard he'd had at the end of the drive.

'Well, have a seat.' She sat down on one of the hardback chairs and watched him uneasily, conscious of all that had passed between them on the trail. He looked so large in the living-room, as if he should be outside, as if the inside of the house was too constraining.

He eased himself on the big overstuffed chair near the window and watched her. His eyes narrowed slightly as he studied her, taking in the soft flush to her cheeks, the vulnerability around her mouth, her hair pulled back for coolness, displaying her slender neck.

'I had a surprise when I got in last night,' she said for something to say when the silence stretched out. 'Dr Watson has offered me a partnership.'

Cache's eyebrow rose and he looked at her patiently. 'And?'

'And nothing. I was surprised, that's all. You don't seem to be.'

He shrugged, looked at his hat turning gently in his hands. He'd spoken to Doc Watson only a couple of weeks ago. Holly was good, and he'd told him so. He hadn't known what the doc had in mind when he'd asked about Holly.

'Are you going to take it?'

She shook her head slowly. 'I don't think so. I'm returning to Kentucky, remember.'

'I remember you saying that.' His voice was neutral, his expression bland. 'But are you sure of your reception?' he reminded her.

'I'm sure my uncle will let me work at Windmere Farms.' The uncertainty showed in her tone and she frowned. He'd asked that of her before. Why was he throwing doubts on her plan? What did he hope to accomplish? She didn't need to share her misgivings with Cache. Uncle Tyson had been rigid in his decision before, but surely time would have mellowed him. The fact that she was a practising vet should change his mind. It had to!

'Easy enough to find out; why not call him? If there's no job there, you might want to consider Doc Watson's offer. No sense in burning bridges if you don't need to.'

The suggestion was reasonable. Holly glanced at the phone for a moment then at Cache.

'Maybe. I'll see.'

'Call now,' he ordered.

She was uncertain. Uncertain of her reception. What if her uncle wouldn't let her work for Windmere Farms? She wasn't sure a phone call would work. She had thought to show up and convince him.

'I think I'll go visit. I can talk about it then, see how he feels now.' After seven years, surely he'd at least listen to her. Give her a chance.

'Doc probably wants an answer soon. Give your uncle a call, Holly.' Cache's eyes were dark blue, his jaw stubborn. Obviously a man to be obeyed. That was how he built up his ranch, she thought. People listened to him.

'OK.'

She took a deep breath and moved to dial the long, familiar number. Anticipation built; what would she find when someone answered? Should she wait until night? Disconnect and fly home as originally planned?

Her uncle answered on the fourth ring. He was surprised to hear from her and the first few minutes of the conversation were spent in catching up on the news of her cousins. When Holly broached the subject of her return, and possibly working at Windmere Farms, she was shocked at her uncle's response.

She could see Cache's attention as he carefully observed her reactions.

'I can't believe it... But Uncle Tyson... Yes, I understand that.' She was quiet a long time, listening to the voice on the line. 'Sure, it's your decision. I'll write you about my job here. Tell the boys hi for me.' Slowly she placed the receiver on its cradle.

Turning to Cache, her eyes wide and shocked, she shook her head. 'How did you know?' she whispered.

'Know what? What was the outcome?' He leaned forward, but remained seated.

'There will be no job at Windmere. There's not going to be a Windmere any more. He's selling it to Runningmede, to merge the two.' Holly sank back in her chair, feeling numb. For as long as she could remember she had wanted to work with her uncle and cousins at Windmere Farms. Now that would never be possible. She'd been gone too long. Left it too late. She couldn't believe it.

'Holly?' Cache moved to hunker down beside her, taking her hands in his. They were like ice.

'Honey, are you OK?' His blue eyes mirrored his concern.

She nodded, gazing down at him, hurt and confusion obvious in her eyes. 'I'm just . . . numb, I guess. He's sold the farm. He's retiring and going travelling, around the world. My cousins are set in their jobs. I . . . it's the last thing I expected to hear.' She stared off into space, still unable to believe what her uncle had told her.

He would settle some money on her, he'd told her. As if she had wanted anything like that. He still didn't understand her. She'd wanted to be a part of the family farm, have a part in working with the horses. Now she would never get the chance.

'Hey, Holly, it's not the end of the world. There's always Doc's offer.'

She stared at him. Cache would like her to stay around, she was sure. It would only be a matter of time, then, before she succumbed to his pressure. Dear God, she loved it when he kissed her, teased her, just spent time with her. But then what?

Her hands were tingling as he caressed the backs of them gently, his thumbs circling across her skin. She drew back. Time to end this before it led into something she couldn't handle today. She needed time to think things through. She felt as if the world had tilted on its axis. What was she going to do? All her thoughts for the future would have to change.

'I think you should go now, Cache,' she said softly, tugging her hands free. 'I need to think about what I want to do.' She wanted to be alone. The change in everything was just too much to take in at once.

He rose and clamped his hat back on. 'Let me know what you decide.'

'I'm sure you'll hear.' She rose and led the way to the door.

'Wait a minute; what do you mean?'

She turned and looked up at him, her eyes wide with innocence. 'Why, only that if I stay you'll soon enough know it. The whole town gossips, doesn't it?'

'I'd rather hear it from you, darlin'.'

Holly smiled smugly up at him; he didn't like someone holding back. He liked to be in charge. But he would find out she didn't jump to his bidding. She realised her mistake when his eyes darkened and he lowered his head to hers.

She ducked away and pushed at him. 'Please just leave, Cache. I have patients due here any minute.' The afternoon office hours were about to start. She didn't need to add any fuel to gossip. Especially if there was any chance of her staying on in Waxco.

'And I'd hate to start something I couldn't finish.'

'Right. Goodbye, Cache.'

'Call me and let me know,' he repeated.

She watched as he drove away, then turned back to the house, wondering what she should do. What she *could* do. Though was there any choice? She had a job offer, a place she liked. And where she could be near that frustrating cowboy who disturbed her life. But was it enough?

Over the next several days Holly went about her work quietly, assessing if Waxco was where she wanted to put down roots, or whether she should return to Kentucky and seek other opportunities there. It was odd, after so long, to lose her goal. For years she'd planned to return home in triumph, winning the approval of her uncle and working at Windmere Farms. She felt adrift, indecisive, mixed up. What should she do?

Yet she couldn't stay in this state of limbo for long. She needed to make some decision and move on. Right or wrong, something had to be decided, and soon.

Friday she awoke with a decision made. She'd stay in Waxco. She'd write to Dr Watson today and accept his kind offer, then start looking for a place to stay. By the time the Watsons returned home, she'd be ready to move to her new place. She felt a weight lift—and wondered why she had thought the decision so difficult.

But how would it affect her relationship with Cache?

Cache had phoned her each night, and invited her over each evening to talk to him. She wasn't ready to face him and had put him off. This afternoon she'd drive out to the Lone Tree and let him know her decision. She wondered how he would take the news.

She hurried through her calls and prayed there would be no emergencies. She didn't want to put off telling him, now that she'd decided.

The day was breezy and a little cool when Holly set off for the ranch. She had grabbed a sweatshirt before leaving home and knew she'd need it before the day was over. The drive was familiar and before long she turned before the barn and pulled up.

It was quiet, a couple of horses in the corral dozing in the afternoon sun, small dust whirlwinds swirling in the breeze. She saw no one. The ranch seemed empty, hot in the clear summer day.

'Howdy, Doc,' Sam called to her from near the house; he'd heard her jeep. She smiled and waited for him as he hurried across the yard towards her.

'Hi, Sam, Cache around?'

'Nope, went out just after breakfast, riding towards the west range, going to check on the cattle over there. He thought there might be a fence down somewhere. Should be back soon. Want to wait?'

'Maybe I'll hang around for a while.'

'Sally Lambert is up at the house; you could join her,' he said slyly.

Holly wrinkled her nose and shook her head. 'I don't think so. I'll check out Starlight and see how he's doing. See Beau. If Cache's not back by then, I'll come another time.'

'You might go riding, catch him on the range.' Sam fell into step beside her as she entered the cool barn.

'Or I could miss him entirely—it's a big open range. It's not that important; I'll see him another time.' She certainly didn't want to tell him her news with Sally hanging around. What was she doing here anyway? Would he think she was chasing him the way Sally did? She should have waited and let him learn through the town gossip. Why give him any reason to think his bossy ways had impact on her? She didn't have to jump to his orders the way his ranch hands did.

She crossed to the stall where the foal was housed and looked through the bars at him. 'He looks fine; eating well?' She stroked his velvety muzzle when he ambled over to see her, curiosity strong.

'Yeah, getting spoiled; everyone watches out for him. Shame about his ma.' Sam rested his foot on the lower railing and watched the little horse.

'Cache bought that mare for Trish,' she remembered.

'Yeah, and Trish really loved her. It was when they were first married, and things were still OK. Think the boss always thought of the good days when he saw that mare.'

'Cache told me Trish was leaving when she was killed,' Holly said slowly, her fingers rubbing against the foal's head.

'Well, I wished she'd been killed a mite earlier,' Sam said, his voice hard.

That surprised Holly; she swung around to stare at the old man.

'Why?'

'Before she and her venomous tongue ruined a good man. Cache tried hard to make that marriage work. He gave her so much, and she told him he couldn't make a woman happy. He took it to heart, and never married. What this place needs is a woman and lots of kids.'

'Hey, Sam, come quick,' a panicked voice called from the yard.

Sam turned and ran from the barn, Holly right on his heels. She stopped at the door as one of the cowhands was trying to catch Roman. The big horse was lathered with sweat, his saddle empty.

'Where's Cache?' Holly heard Sam ask, her eyes were riveted to the saddle. Dark, rusty stains covered the side. The horse was cut, blood dripping from his side.

She hurried over and reached for one of the reins just as Sam got him under control.

'Don't know,' said the cowhand; 'just saw the horse running and tried to get him.'

Holly felt Roman's side. There were two gored areas, the blood-flow slowing. Her eyes were drawn again and again to the saddle. Roman's blood hadn't flowed there.

'Damned longhorn, I bet,' Sam said. 'I'll try to backtrack him; Frank, you call Doc Bellingham and tell him to stand by; we may need him.'

'Wait, Sam, I want to come, too.' Holly looked at the horse one more time. She thought he'd be OK until she could get back. But if Cache was hurt, she wanted to be with him!

'OK, bring your bag, Doc; who knows what we'll find?' Sam hurried into the barn. He was back in no time with two horses. Holly had grabbed her bag and sweatshirt and was giving hasty instructions to the cowboy about Roman. She turned and tied her black bag on to the saddle and vaulted into the seat.

'He probably just got tossed,' Sam said as they kicked the horses.

Holly hoped with all her heart that it was so, but feared more.

CHAPTER TEN

HOLLY'S heart pounded with fear as she and Sam followed the trail past the house and beyond. Where was Cache? Was he all right, or was that his blood on the saddle? As they crested the ridge behind the homestead, Sam slowed a little and started looking at the ground, trying to see the direction Roman had come from. Holly trusted that the old cowboy knew what he was doing and could lead them to Cache.

She was fearful of what they would find, however. Cache was a good rider; to have fallen could mean he was seriously injured. Or worse. She refused to let herself consider that. He had to be all right. *He had to*!

She followed Sam, staying behind him so as not to interfere, her own eyes searching the horizon, wanting to find Cache and assure herself he was fine. They would probably find him walking along, cussing that old horse for dumping him. And wouldn't she love to tease him about that. She refused to think of anything worse.

Holly's throat ached, and she had trouble swallowing. She couldn't imagine her world without Cache. He meant everything to her. With startling realisation, she blinked. She *loved* the man. He was infuriating, patronising and afraid to make a commitment to another woman, but it didn't matter. She loved him! Maybe he'd never love her, but she didn't care at that moment. Her life would be incomplete without him. He had to be all right!

With that knowledge, it became more imperative to her that they locate him soon. She had to make sure he was fine.

She was almost screaming with impatience and frustration. Why couldn't Sam find him? Her eyes searched the landscape, looking for something out of the ordinary. Some sign of Cache. But she saw only the bleached grass, the scattered rocks and the occasional live oak that dotted the range. In the distance, she could see cattle. But no sign of Cache.

Where was he? Time dragged, minutes seemed endless as they slowly rode over the range, covering ground they thought Roman had traversed. Here and there splashes of blood were drying in the dirt. Sam would draw up and study the ground, pausing each time he found a drop of blood. Searching for more signs, searching for Cache.

'I think I see him.' Sam spurred his horse and took off, Holly in quick pursuit, her eyes frantically trying to see what Sam had seen.

And there he was, leaning against a small boulder, his head back, hat off and eyes closed. He didn't stir as the two rode up and hastily dismounted. Sam reached him first.

'Cache?'

Holly stopped and stared at him. She was breathless, as if hit in the stomach. There was blood all over his left leg, soaking into the ground. An ineffective attempt had been made to staunch the flow using his bandanna. But blood still seeped out.

His hat was several feet away, too far for Cache to reach it, and the blazing sun beat relentlessly down on his exposed face.

Holly's training took over. Quickly assessing the problem, she determined that he had been gored by a longhorn, like his horse. She glanced around quickly to see if the steer was still around, but saw nothing. Yanking her bag off the saddle, she snatched up his hat in passing and hurried over to him.

Sam was testing for vital signs, looking at the leg.

'How is he?' She knelt beside him, her heart pounding in fear; the pallor of his face was dreadful.

Please God, let him be alive!

'Pretty bad, I think. Look at all the blood. I'll ride for the ranch, get the medi-evac helicopter out. You stay with him, Doc.' Sam looked at Holly, his eyes worried.

She nodded confidently. 'Sure, I'll take good care of him. Hurry, Sam, but don't go getting hurt yourself on the way.'

She was already reaching for Cache's wrist as Sam mounted and started off. She sought a pulse. It was light, thready. His breathing was shallow. She knew he was in shock. Scrambling over to her horse, she snatched her sweatshirt from the saddle and hurried back. Each second seemed endless. Hurry, Sam, she urged.

While her heart was frantic with worry, she moved with calm efficiency. Laying Cache down on the rocky ground, she drew near a couple of flat rocks to elevate his feet, covering him with the sweatshirt, wishing she had a blanket. She set his hat gently on his head to shelter it from the sun and quickly opened her bag. There must be something she could do for him; she had to stop the bleeding.

When she looked back, he had his eyes opened, just a crack, but she was relieved to see he was conscious.

'Oh, Cache, are you all right?' Stupid question, she could see he was hurt, but her mind couldn't think.

'Am now, darlin'.' His voice was low, faint.

She nodded and tried to smile. Time to check the makeshift bandage he'd used. He had wadded up his bandanna to hold on his leg, but the pressure had eased when he fell unconscious.

'You've lost a lot of blood.' She cut away some of the jeans so that she could see the wound more clearly. The sun was hot on her back, and she felt small and lonely in the vast land with the injured man depending upon her. But her hands were steady, and her voice firm. She was a professional, and could keep her personal feelings from showing when the task demanded it.

'Feel light-headed,' he mumbled, his eyes riveted on her.

'Don't wonder. Hold still; I want to see if...' She examined the wound, appalled at the amount of blood still flowing. The wound was ragged, a bit dirty and the blood-flow wasn't slowing. It looked as if the steer had nicked an artery.

She bit her lip and looked at him in indecision. 'Cache, you're still bleeding pretty bad. How long ago did this happen?' She pressed a pad to the wound, leaning against him to apply pressure, trying desperately to staunch the flow.

'Don't know. Tried to make it home with Roman; he was hurt too. Blacked out, I guess. Fix me up, darlin'.'

'I'm a horse doctor, not a people doctor.' The pad was slowly turning bright red.

'A vein's a vein whether you're a horse or a man. Holly, if you don't do something I could bleed to death.' His voice sounded weaker.

She nodded, knowing that was probably true. She glanced around in despair at the blood already soaking into the thirsty ground. How much had he already lost? She checked her watch. Sam would not even be at the

ranch yet. How much longer before she could expect the
medi-evac helicopter?

She glanced at him again. His breathing was shallow.
Her mind raced. She knew she had to do something to
save him. But dared she?

Reaching a decision, she turned to her bag and drew
out the sutures from her case. Her hands shook slightly,
but she knew he was right. The bleeding had to stop or
he'd die.

She cut more of the jeans around the wound, high up
on his thigh, and heard him chuckle. She glanced up,
met his eyes, marvelling that he could find anything
amusing at this time. Her heart turned over when her
eyes locked with his. She loved him so much she ached
with it!

'I wanted...to get your pants...off, never thought
of...you cutting mine...off.'

She gave him a speaking glance and filled a syringe
with pain-killer; the man had a one-track mind.

'I don't know about this, Cache. I know how to do
it for large animals. I think this will numb the area for
the sutures, but I'm not sure. Anyway, I don't want to
wait any longer.' She was proud of her firm voice. She
didn't want to frighten him.

'Hey, one animal's...pretty much the same as
any...other. Anyway, I think you're...right not to wait.'

Was his voice getting weaker?

Holly administered the local anaesthetic, waited a
minute for it to take effect, then began closing the
wound. She found the source of the bleeding and shut
it off. Her hands were steady, her mind occupied with
the work at hand; she refused to think that it was Cache
she was working on. Nor of the ramifications should
anyone press charges. She was a vet, for God's sake, not

a physician. But if she didn't do this, he'd die, she was sure of it.

He passed out before she was finished. But she continued working, competently and efficiently, refusing to think about Cache, refusing to think of anything except the procedure at hand. She closed off the nick in the artery, closing the wound and packing it in bandages.

When finished, she sank back on the ground, her hands trembling and her stomach churning. She swallowed a couple of times and looked up to clear her eyes of the tears that threatened. Oh, God, she hoped she did everything right. 'Please don't let him die,' she breathed.

'Cache?' she called his name softly. She felt for his pulse; it was slow, weak. His breathing was steady, however.

'Come on, Cache, wake up.' She brushed the hair from his forehead, her fingers trailing through the thickness. He was so still.

'Cache, don't you die on me, do you hear me, you dumb cowboy?' She shook him a little, fear rising like bile in her throat.

He lay so still, she checked again to make sure he was still breathing.

'Dammit, Cache, wake up. Don't die on me, you can't die.' Tears welled up and she impatiently dashed them away.

'I love you, you dumb cowboy. Don't you dare die. I'm staying in Waxco, and you better be here for me. Do you hear me? Oh, Cache, please hear me.'

'I hear you, darlin'.' His voice was faint, his eyes remained closed. 'No good staying...'

'Of course it is. I'll be the best vet this town ever saw. Stay with me, Cache.' Her hands held his tightly, her strength willed him to stay conscious. Where was that helicopter? She scanned the sky, saw nothing.

'Don't love me, Holly,' he said, his eyes opening a slit.

'Why? I can love who I want. And I want you, Cache.'

'Never work...' He closed his eyes.

'Yes, it would, damn you! I'm not Trish. You know that. Think on it, Cache. I'm not Trish, and you can't lump us together. I've lived here for weeks now and know about all about it. I'm not going to pine for the city, for shopping and nightclubs and travelling. I've been on cattle drives, not just yours, others, too. Trish and I are not alike. You're just being stubborn. Do you love me?'

He was silent.

'Oh, my love, don't die, hold on, Sam's gone for help, hold on. It will be OK.' She cradled his hand in hers, hugging it to her breasts, willing life into him, willing him to hold on and not die.

'Yes.' The word was whispered.

But yes what? Yes, he loved her? Or yes, he'd hold on? She kissed his hand; he had to live, he simply had to! She loved him so much, and she wanted him to love her. But if he didn't, she still needed him to live, to be a part of her life.

She glanced at his leg; the bandages were still white; thank God the bleeding had stopped. But he'd lost so much blood. Would he make it? She couldn't bear it if he died.

Where was that damned helicopter?

'Roman?'

She looked at him. He was hovering near death and was worried about his horse.

'He's fine. Frank's watching him. I checked him, he'll be fine.' She kept her tone positive. She didn't want him worrying about the horse. She'd see to him as soon as she knew Cache was safe. Tears slid down her cheeks. She was so afraid. So alone and afraid. It was a big country, needed big people to live in it, and she felt so insignificant.

He opened his eyes a little, a small smile tugging at his lips. 'Your... bedside manner leaves a lot to be desired. The last time...you cried was when a horse died... Am I dying?'

She brushed at her tears with the back of one hand, still clasping his against her breast. She shook her head. 'No, you're not. You're too stubborn to die from some dumb old cow.'

'Steer, darlin', goddam ornery old longhorn steer.' For a moment his voice had a familiar teasing ring.

'I knew that,' she whispered, her hands gripping him, delighted that he could answer back. Maybe he would be OK. She scanned the sky again. Nothing.

'You're so pretty, honey. You should be... doing teas and going to the opera...to dances.' His voice was getting softer; he spoke more slowly.

She shook her head, tears still slipping down. 'I like Grange dances and camping out, and riding hard and fast. I like the open range land of California, and small towns where the people like you if you do your job well.'

She looked up; she heard something. The whomp whomp of the helicopter. She searched the sky; there, she saw it coming over the hill and flying low.

'Help's almost here, Cache,' she said excitedly.

'You were my help,' he mumbled before falling unconscious again.

In only a moment the big medi-evac helicopter settled down some distance away, its blades slowing as it kicked up dust and rocks. Before the blades fully stopped, two paramedics jumped down and hurried over to Holly. Sam was right behind them.

In only a few minutes, Holly and Cache were lifting off in the helicopter and Sam was riding her horse back to the ranch. Holly squeezed into the corner of the helicopter and watched as the paramedics administered plasma and took Cache's vital signs. She wanted some indication from the men that Cache would be OK, but she could tell nothing from their sporadic conversation. It was out of her hands now; she could only pray she'd done enough.

Dr Bellingham met the helicopter at the county hospital. He greeted Holly and directed her to the nearby waiting-room, his attention all for Cache. She sank down in one of the chairs, noticing for the first time the blood on her jeans and shirt. Cache's blood. Slowly she rose and found a washroom to clean up in. It all seemed unreal. Only, she knew it wasn't. Was he going to be all right?

The wait was endless. After a while she was joined by Sam. But she didn't know how long she sat there. He brought her some coffee and she sipped at it, just for something to do. Her heart and soul was in limbo until she heard how Cache was doing.

Dr Bellingham walked into the waiting-room, a big smile on his face. He nodded to Sam and spoke to Holly.

'Well, if Doc Watson doesn't want you for a partner, come see me. You did a fine job on Cache. Saved his life, I reckon. Another pint of blood gone and he'd be dead.'

'But he's OK now?'

'I think he will be. We pumped a little blood in him, checked him over. We'll know better in the morning. We'll monitor his vitals all night. Go home, Holly; you did a wonderful thing, but there is nothing further to be done. He should be awake tomorrow; you can come back and see him then.' The doctor's voice was gentle, his smile kindly but his tone firm. She might as well go home. She nodded, drained.

'I'll give you a ride home, Doc,' Sam said, twisting his hat in his hand.

'No, take me to the ranch first, Sam. I want to check Roman, make sure he's OK,' Holly said. She'd promised Cache. Besides, her jeep was there.

It was after midnight by the time Holly reached home. Roman had required a couple of stitches and a thorough cleaning. She'd instructed the cowhands to keep him in the stall for a few days. He'd be fine by then. She only hoped Cache would be well as quickly.

She was utterly tired. Holly held off until she was in bed, but then gave way to the tears of relief that had threatened since Dr Bellingham had said Cache should be safe. Over and over she relived the fear of the afternoon, the fear when she'd seen him so unlike his normal robust, sexy self. But the doctor had said he'd be fine. She had to hold on to that thought. The tears flowed for a long time.

Holly spent a restless night and awoke early. She waited impatiently until eight o'clock when she could call the hospital. The nurse who answered informed her that Cache had spent a comfortable night and the doctor was with him now. She had not yet heard if the doctor was permitting visitors. Perhaps Holly could check back later?

Holly hung up the phone, certain that Dr Bellingham would let her see Cache; he'd as much as said so last night. She'd wait for Emmie, tell her what had happened and then go to the hospital.

Holly ate a hasty breakfast, and was just washing the dishes when the phone rang. Thinking it was Dr Bellingham, she dashed to grab it before the second ring, anxious to hear the latest about Cache.

'Holly, Stan Connors, vet over at Overilla. I've got a problem, need your help.'

'What's up?' Her eyes glanced impatiently at the clock. Almost nine; Emmie should be here soon. She would update Emmie and then leave for the hospital first thing.

'...so I'm not sure but I think it's anthrax.'

Holly's attention focused on what Stan was saying. She'd missed the first part, but her attention was caught by the dreaded word anthrax. The disease could go through a herd in no time, wiping it out, spreading to neighbouring ranches.

'Tell me again,' she said, her attention fully on Stan.

He was still unsure, but the symptoms sounded classic. He wanted her help in isolating the animals, analysing the disease and taking steps to make sure it didn't spread if it was anthrax.

'I'm on my way,' she said, her mind spinning with everything she needed to take. She wished Emmie would hurry up. She needed to tell her about Cache, see if she'd go and visit Cache for her, explain why she couldn't come herself today.

It wasn't satisfactory, but it would have to do, Holly thought a short time later when she was driving over to Overilla to meet Stan. She wanted to see for herself that Cache was all right, but she trusted Dr Bellingham to do his job, and she had to do hers.

For four days Holly worked harder than she had ever done. She and Stan did indeed find anthrax in some of the cattle. Harry Barnard, the rancher with the affected cattle, had just brought in a dozen breeder stock from Texas. These had been carrying the disease.

By the end of four days, they'd isolated all infected animals, and put them down. The rest of the herd was inoculated, the affected pasture closed until it could be cleaned—an expensive and time-consuming project. Fortunately they'd caught the disease in time to prevent major damage to Barnard's herd, and prevented spread to any other ranches. They'd keep his herd in isolation for a few more weeks, but the worst was behind them.

The calls were numerous once the word spread and Emmie and Dr Connors' assistant spent long hours on the phone reassuring everyone. This was cattle country, and everyone was concerned about the threat of anthrax.

When Holly reached home the night of the fourth day, she checked her desk for the messages Emmie left her each day on Cache's progress. It was her only link to him. She had got up early each day, been gone long hours. He was asleep when she'd called the first night. After that, she hadn't tried, but relied on the notes that Emmie left for her. It had not been satisfactory, but she'd had no choice.

'Cache fine,' Emmie had written. Holly shook her head and headed for bed. She would have liked a little more than just that, but Emmie didn't necessarily know that. It was a frustrating way to communicate, but Holly didn't have a better one.

The next morning she called the hospital, hoping to talk to Cache.

'Sorry, Dr Murphy, Cache checked out yesterday afternoon. He's home now,' the cheerful voice said.

Holly's spirits lightened. She'd see to her patients and then go out and visit him. He must be doing fine for Dr Bellingham to have released him.

It was late when she finished everything, too late to drive to the Lone Tree and visit a convalescent. Frustration was driving her wild. Dammit, tomorrow, sick animals or not, she was going to see Cache!

The next afternoon, calling a halt to her list, she stopped in town for a bouquet of flowers, then headed to the Long Tree. She couldn't believe it was six days since she'd last seen him. Six endless days. She needed to see him, reassure herself he was doing OK; listen to his teasing, have him kiss her.

She licked her lips, tasting him in her mind. She couldn't wait for him to kiss her again. Surely he'd give her at least one kiss. If only for saving his life.

When she drew up near the barn, she saw the pick-up Sally Lambert used. Her heart sank. Was she here? Taking a deep breath, Holly gathered her flowers and walked up to the house. The day was warm, the sun bright in a cloudless blue sky, and the scent of horses, hot dust and the sage from the hills mingled to remind Holly of the cattle drive, the rides she and Cache had made, the fright she'd had the day she and Sam had found him.

Sally must have seen her drive up; she came to the door, and slipped through.

'Cache is resting now. I can tell him you came by,' she said, blocking the doorway.

'I could wait,' Holly said, still holding the flowers before her.

'I wouldn't if I were you. It could be hours. Want me to call you when he wakes up?' Sally asked.

Holly stared at her, then smiled. 'Would you?'

Sally looked flustered, then shrugged. She reached for the flowers. 'No point in waiting; he's asleep.'

'You're waiting,' Holly said.

'Actually, Dr Murphy, I've been helping out. Since you're an outsider, you might not realise how we all help each other out in emergencies. Cache and I have something special between us so of course I'd help him out when he needs it. He knows where you live; if he'd wanted to see you, he could have called or sent one of the men.'

Holly stared at her for a moment, struck by what Sally had said. She nodded and gave up, her heart sinking a little. Much as she hated to admit it, the girl was right. Cache had been well enough to go home yesterday. If he'd wanted to talk to her, he could have called. She wouldn't start something with Cache still convalescent. He knew where she was. If he wanted to see her, he could call her.

Her face burning with embarrassment, she tried a polite smile, and felt as if her face would crack. Cache was probably glad she had not come earlier. How awful to have someone say they loved you if you didn't love them back. And she wouldn't meet him before Sally for anything.

'I'll check on Roman, then, and be off. Do tell him I came to see him,' she said, knowing the chances of that were probably slim. But did it really matter? Cache had never indicated that he wanted anything more than a casual fling. He had always thought she'd be leaving soon for Kentucky. Holly had been so adamant about that, he thought he could count on it. Now she was staying. How awkward for him.

She hoped he hadn't heard all her babbling when he had been so injured. If he hadn't, she'd be able to forget it, pretend it hadn't happened and stay. Otherwise, she couldn't remain in Waxco after all. She couldn't stay where she wasn't wanted. And she'd be too embarrassed to face him again, if that were the case.

She'd been a fool. Cache didn't want to make any kind of commitment to a woman, and if he did, why look further than Sally Lambert? He'd known her all her life, knew what kind of wife she'd make, knew she was used to this kind of life. She wouldn't long for the city as Trish had done.

Even that day on the range, Cache had told Holly to go back to dances and tea. As if that interested her. He didn't know her at all, and didn't seem to want to. Her spirits dropped a little lower.

She found the barn deserted, except for Starlight in one stall and Roman in the adjacent one.

'Hi, guys,' she said softly, glad to see both doing so well. She slipped into Roman's stall to examine him. He was doing fine, almost completely healed.

Then she went to visit Starlight. He was growing despite the loss of his mother. Someone was doing something right. She watched him for a few moments, her spirits lightened a little bit by his antics. He was so adorable.

Time was passing, and there was nothing more for Holly to do. She left the barn, and slowly headed for the jeep. Time to go home and put her life in some sort of order. Everything was changing so fast and she had better be prepared to deal with it.

'Holly!'

She turned. Cache was crossing the ground from the house, hobbling on crutches. Holly stared and a smile started as she saw him. Slowly she walked towards him, her eyes never leaving his. He'd obviously dressed hastily—he was barefoot, jeans on and zipped, a shirt drawn on but not buttoned. Her heart began beating heavily in her chest as she walked to the man she loved.

CHAPTER ELEVEN

'How are you doing?' Holly asked, breathless as she came up to him. God, she was glad to see him up and about; he'd been so close to death. Now he looked as cocky as ever. She couldn't help smiling broadly.

He stopped and rested on the crutches, his eyes blazing blue down at her, taking in the soft brown hair, the brandy coloured eyes gazing back at him so trustingly. His lips tilted in his lop-sided grin.

'I'm doing fine. Should be riding again in a day or two.' The soft drawl was music to Holly's ears.

'No!' It was too soon.

He chuckled. 'No, it'll be a few weeks, according to Doc Bellingham.'

'I should hope so! But not according to you?' She knew him; a few weeks would be too long. He'd chafe at the inactivity.

'Hey, I'm up, walking and doing fine. A week or so's all I need.'

'I was so afraid...' She trailed off, unable to stop her hand from reaching out to touch him, running her hand lightly down his arm, feeling the heat of him through the light cotton of the shirt, as if her touch could re-assure her that he was alive and would be fine. Her eyes were drawn to his chest revealed through the open shirt. She felt herself grow warm as she fought the longing to rest her head against him, to be drawn into his arms, to feel his lips on hers again.

'Cache, what are you doing out of bed? Dr Bellingham said you needed rest, bed-rest.' Sally came hurrying out of the house and down the path like an irate nurse.

'I'm fine, Sally, don't hover,' he said without looking away from Holly.

When Sally reached them she glared at Holly, turned to Cache, her features softening. 'Come on back, Cache; she can come in to visit, if you're up to it.'

'I'm up to it.' His eyes were still fixed on Holly. She felt as if she was drowning in the sensations, the deep blue gaze holding her as if he'd never left her go.

'Run along, Sally, this is grown-up stuff,' Cache said as the girl hovered near by.

'Cache.' She looked at Holly, her eyes angry, but bafflement soon replaced anger.

'I appreciate your help, Sally. And your dad's. But I've got someone who can help me now in ways you never could.' He raised an eyebrow at Holly. 'Right?' he asked softly.

She nodded, too afraid to speak. Was he saying what she wanted to hear, or was she imagining it?

Sally waited a moment, then left, but neither Holly nor Cache noticed.

'I owe you my life, Doc Bellingham said,' he said, shifting slightly on the crutches.

She shrugged. 'I'm glad I was able to do something. I was so afraid that day. You lost a lot of blood, you know.' She didn't want to be talking about that awful day. She wanted to hear more about why he'd sent Sally away. And how she could help him in ways Sally never could.

'Yeah, and, much as I hate to admit it, Sally's right— I need to get back inside.'

Holly giggled slightly, relieved that the tension was easing. 'I should think so, rushing out here barefoot and half dressed. Weren't you in bed?'

'Yes, but when I heard you I wanted to see you and Sally wasn't exactly encouraging. I didn't have time to waste. Weren't you ready to leave?'

'You could have called me; I would have come back out,' she said gently.

She walked with him back up the path, held the screen door open for him. With a quick glance around, she saw Sally pulling away, the dust kicked up behind her truck drifting on the still air before settling back on the baked earth.

Cache sank on the sofa and tossed the crutches down with a clatter. 'A few more days and I won't need them, but the good doctor doesn't want the stitches to pull out. Your stitches, as I hear.'

Holly sat gingerly near him on the sofa, watching him warily. Tension began to fill the room and she wondered what he was going to say.

He leaned back and watched her, his eyes narrowed. 'Want to tell me why this is the first time I've seen you since the day of the accident?' he said, his voice calm, even. But Holly wondered at the slight tightening of his lips.

She shrugged, trying not to let her hopes rise too much at his question, wanting to launch herself into his arms, cover him with kisses and have him tell her he loved her. She shook her head at that notion. He'd never given her any reasons to suspect he felt the same way she did. He just wanted an affair.

'Didn't Emmie tell you?'

He shook his head. 'I didn't see Emmie. I only wanted to see you. I didn't have any visitors, except Sam. I wasn't really feeling up to it.'

'She told me each day you were doing better. I...never mind that. I was over at Overilla, helping Stan. We had an outbreak of anthrax.' She looked at him, so glad he was on the mend.

He whistled softly, his face grim. 'Bad?'

'No, we caught it early. Harry Barnard lost fifty head all told. He'd just bought some cattle from Texas, and they were infected. I wanted to come see you, but it was so late each night by the time I got home. Then when I finally did call the hospital you'd already gone home. So here I am.' She smiled shyly, trying to gauge his re-action. Had he heard her that day? Would he let her down easily, or be blunt as he'd been with Sally?

'Holly, out on the range you said you loved me. In fact, you were quite specific about loving me, and that I was not to die.' His eyes held hers, amusement lurking in their depths at the memory.

She closed her eyes in embarrassment. His finger tapped her chin, and she opened her eyes to stare into his. The laughter was gone; they were serious as he looked down at her.

'Remember what I told you, that after Trish I didn't want to try that route again?'

'I remember.' She blinked, trying to keep the tears at bay. She'd confessed her love, and he was reminding her that he wouldn't be tied to a woman again. She felt the ache in her breast, and wished she could push it away. Why had she come today? Nothing had changed, only her feelings for this man. He was the same as always. And he had always been honest with her.

'So was it just the heat of the moment? Why did you tell me that, Holly?'

'Because that's how I feel,' she whispered, unable to lie about it.

'Oh, darlin'.' Cache reached out for her and drew her closer to him, putting one arm around her shoulders and tilting her head up for a kiss. She'd wanted him to kiss her for ages, but not like this, not out of pity!

His lips teased hers then became serious as he deepened the kiss, his tongue caressing her lips, forcing its way past the barrier of her teeth, tracing the soft inner lip, then plunging in her waiting mouth to bring her the satisfaction she knew he alone could give her.

She pushed against him. She didn't want pity from Cache. She wanted to leave. Decide what course to follow and escape with some pride still remaining.

He pulled back after a moment, staring down at her, puzzled. He moved to take her in his arms again, but she pushed against his chest, ignoring the flame of desire that curled within her at the contact of his bare skin against her hands.

'Don't, you'll pull your stitches,' she protested, afraid he'd injure himself again, yet not willing to stay within his embrace.

'Damn, something tells me I'm as close to getting what I want as I've ever been, and I still can't have you.'

'What is it you want, Cache? To sleep with me?'

'Damn straight on that, darlin'.' He dropped a hard kiss on her mouth.

'For the memories?' Exciting memories, was what he'd said? She held on to her tenuous control. She had to get out of here, before she broke down completely. She blinked her eyes again, judging the distance to the door.

'For the sheer pleasure of it, darlin'. Don't you want me?'

She looked up at him, unable to deny it. She loved him so much she'd give almost anything to sleep with him, every night; to wake up with him each day and for them to spend their lives together, sharing, planning, loving.

'Memories aren't enough,' she said slowly, wondering if she should take what he offered. No, that would lead to greater heartbreak down the road.

'Sure are fun, though. We'll have some grand ones to look back on when we're old and grey. Not that I plan to stop making them just because we get old.'

She looked at him, puzzlement showing on her face.

'You know, the Chinese have a saying that if someone saves your life, that life's theirs.'

'You don't owe me anything. And don't laugh at me.' How awful if he felt obligated to her. Her heart squeezed at the thought.

'I think I'm making a mess of this, and that wasn't my intention. Actually, seeing you today threw me off. I thought I could plan this better.'

'What?'

'I'm not laughing at you, darlin'; I remember how I felt when you said that to me. I wanted to deny it, deny how I felt about you. You were leaving, so I thought. It was safe to love you a little, when I knew you'd be going. Then it all changed, and you were staying—and making a strong case why I should consider you and me together.'

Holly watched him, afraid to let her hopes rise. What was he saying?

'But I kept remembering Trish. What I feel for you isn't like what I felt for Trish.'

Holly's heart died a little, but she kept staring at him. She didn't have to be told that.

'Hey.' He saw the hurt in her eyes. 'What I feel for you is stronger, deeper. I'm older now, love, and know myself better. I love you, Holly, more than life itself. If you don't stay, and marry me, I'll just give up. It hurt that I couldn't make a good marriage with Trish. But we just weren't right for each other. I swore off women because of a failed marriage, but looking back I think that was mainly my pride. It's a risk, but one I'm willing to take, if you are, darlin'. Hell, if you don't marry me, I'll die, darlin', just up and die. We could have a good marriage, Holly, I know it.'

Holly couldn't believe her ears. Had he just asked her to marry him?

'Holly?'

'Oh, Cache, I love you!' She flung her arms around his neck, reached up eagerly for his kiss, all thoughts of his injuries forgotten.

'You still didn't answer me,' he said whimsically a few minutes later. Not wanting to stop, he had to nevertheless, before he ignored the doctor's advice and did something to cause damage to his stitches.

'You really didn't ask me anything,' she said, her smile mischievous.

'Holly Murphy, will you do me the honour of becoming my wife?'

'Cache McKendrick, the honour would be all mine; yes, thank you. But are you sure?'

'Darlin', I've been sure since the first day I met you, with those indecent shorts and your feisty attitude. I remember hoping fervently that you weren't the doc's wife.'

'Hah! At least I wasn't some arrogant cowboy, calling everyone "darlin'" when I first met them.'

'But you were my darling, even that first day. You're the only one I've ever called that, darlin'. Not even Trish was as darling as you are.'

'But you kept saying you wouldn't get married again. Why the change of heart? Not that I'm complaining.' She kissed him shyly on the corner of his mouth.

He settled back against the cushions and threaded his fingers through hers, watching their linked hands for a moment. 'It was that damned steer. When Roman took off after we were attacked, and left me on the ground, I really wondered if I'd make it. And I thought about you. What if I'd never see you again?'

He closed his eyes briefly, then glanced at her.

'Then I woke up and you were there, and telling me you loved me. I couldn't believe it. But, once in the hospital, I had doubts. You didn't come, didn't call, didn't try to see me. Had I imagined it? It didn't matter. I knew then I wanted you, more than anything ever in my life. I vowed the next time I saw you I'd find out for sure how you felt, and let you know I love you. And that I'm finally brave enough to risk my heart again to share my life with you.'

Holly's heart glowed with the love she had for Cache. Her dream of so long was gone, replaced with one even better. A practice in a town that was friendly and life with a man who loved her. She was no longer heart-whole and fancy-free. She'd found her true love with Cache McKendrick.

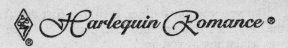

New from Harlequin Romance
a very special six-book series by

The town of Hard Luck, Alaska, needs women!

The O'Halloran brothers, who run a bush-plane service called **Midnight Sons**, are heading a campaign to attract women to Hard Luck. *(Location: north of the Arctic Circle. Population: 150—mostly men!)*

"Debbie Macomber's *Midnight Sons* series is a delightful romantic saga. And each book is a powerful, engaging story in its own right. Unforgettable!"

—Linda Lael Miller

TITLE IN THE MIDNIGHT SONS SERIES:

#3379 BRIDES FOR BROTHERS (available in October 1995)
#3383 THE MARRIAGE RISK (available in November 1995)
#3387 DADDY'S LITTLE HELPER (available in December 1995)
#3395 BECAUSE OF THE BABY (available in February 1996)
#3399 FALLING FOR HIM (available in March 1996)
#3404 ENDING IN MARRIAGE (available in April 1996)

UNLOCK THE DOOR TO GREAT ROMANCE AT BRIDE'S BAY RESORT

Join Harlequin's new across-the-lines series, set in an exclusive hotel on an island off the coast of South Carolina.

Seven of your favorite authors will bring you exciting stories about fascinating heroes and heroines discovering love at Bride's Bay Resort.

Look for these fabulous stories coming to a store near you beginning in January 1996.

Harlequin American Romance #613 in January
Matchmaking Baby by Cathy Gillen Thacker

Harlequin Presents #1794 in February
Indiscretions by Robyn Donald

Harlequin Intrigue #362 in March
Love and Lies by Dawn Stewardson

Harlequin Romance #3404 in April
Make Believe Engagement by Day Leclaire

Harlequin Temptation #588 in May
Stranger in the Night by Roseanne Williams

Harlequin Superromance #695 in June
Married to a Stranger by Connie Bennett

Harlequin Historicals #324 in July
Dulcie's Gift by Ruth Langan

Visit Bride's Bay Resort each month wherever Harlequin books are sold.

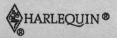

HARLEQUIN ◆ PRESENTS®

Harlequin brings you the best books, by the best authors!

MIRANDA LEE

"...another scandalously sensual winner"
—*Romantic Times*

&

LYNNE GRAHAM

"(Her) strong-willed, hard-loving characters are the sensual
stuff dreams are made of"—*Romantic Times*

Look out next month for:

MISTRESS OF DECEPTION by Miranda Lee
Harlequin Presents #1791

CRIME OF PASSION by Lynne Graham
Harlequin Presents #1792

Harlequin Presents—the best has just gotten better!
Available in February wherever Harlequin books are sold.

TAUTH-5